The Cutmouth Lady

SEMIOTEXT(E) NATIVE AGENTS SERIES
CHRIS KRAUS, EDITOR

The Cutmouth Lady

Romy Ashby

SEMIOTEXT(E) NATIVE AGENTS SERIES

Thank you so much Chris Kraus and Yvonne Shafir
for presenting me with this marvelous opportunity.

I would also like to give thanks to the following:

Carla Leonardi (if ever you visit Seattle, my home town,
go to Cafe Lago and say hello to Carla), the beautiful
songs of Anna Domino, Liza Stelle, Vali Myers,
Loren MacIver, Jill Dunbar and Jenny Feder at
Three Lives in New York, Hilary Sio, Carl Rosen,
Patti Brodbeck, Marilou Carlin, Jacqui Spadaro,
Peter Cohen, Annie West, Billy Leyes, Susan Ward,
Mary Kelley, Gianni Menichetti, Carole Ramer,
Nina Eskridge, Meredith Paige, Connie Santoro,
Larry Camp, Nicole Werner, Mae Skidmore,
Cathy Clarke, Margaret Whittemore, Fran Bonamo,
Greg Baron, Lorraine Schein, Charles Marotta,
Tony Puma, Judy Weinmann, Ivory Freidus,
Carla Olla, Jennifer Holiday, Robin Simmen, and
John Carafoli. Thanks to Liz Harvey, for her generous
help, and bless you, POU.

Semiotext(e) gratefully acknowledges the assistance of
the New York State Council on the Arts Literature
Program in the publication of this book.

Back Cover Photo: Carla Leonardi
Book Design: Annie West

Semiotext(e) Offices

522 Philosophy Hall	POB 568
Columbia University	Williamsburgh Station
New York, NY 10027	Brooklyn, NY 11211

Phone & Fax: 718-963-2603

Printed in the United States of America

"We loved to creep through the undergrowth
to a knoll direct behind their house,
and lying on our stomachs in the
hazelbrush, watch Mrs. K. smoke
her villainous little corncob pipe."

—Loyse K. Chapman,
the girl who was my grandma

this little book is for her

CONTENTS

THE CUTMOUTH LADY

I can remember three crimes from that enchanted and tormented Spring. There was the sushi man, who stabbed people with an ice pick on the packed blueline train, and there was the poisoner, who left devastated coca colas open in telephone booths. And then there was Kuchisake Onna, the cutmouth lady, the only one of those three (although I could never really consider her a criminal) who brought a tremor into my dreams.

One day she just came, and then suddenly it was as if there were cutmouth ladies all over Japan, springing up and tearing off their surgical masks in front of children. On television I saw the place where the first encounter had occurred. A narrow lane along the reedy lake, near a little grey boat rental house. There was a cluster of soft drink vending machines, which looked unreal and sinister in the grim, drab light, and it had been at these vending machines where the cutmouth lady waited early Monday morning. I remember this clearly, because it was the day after the big kite festival. Along came three children with their red leather school satchels. One of them carried a bucket of live eels. This was a region famous for eels.

In the wet mist of early morning, there materialized a woman over by the boat rental house. She stood at the vending machines, dropping a coin into one. She was dressed properly, as if she might be on her way to Fuji Bank, just over the bridge. One of the children would later describe her as having worn a dress by Hanae Mori, with gold buttons.

Then there was the white cotton surgical style mask, but this in itself had no startling effect. Many people, especially during flu season, wore such masks over their nose and mouth. This woman was entirely unremarkable; she might have been anyone. The only questionable issue was what she was doing down this lonely, marshy lane so early in the morning. The children knew all of the neighbors, and this lady was not one of them. When they were quite close to her, she called out.

"Excuse me!"

The children stopped. She walked toward them, and in her muffled voice asked them,

"Do you think I am pretty?"

They assessed her. No question from an adult was ever entirely unexpected. The children all agreed that she was pretty. Even with her face partially obscured by the mask it was still obvious that this was a pretty woman. They could not see the sadness swarming around her like thick, green moths, while they stood looking up at her, in their school clothes and sneakers, there at the little curve in the lane where the vending machines hummed.

"Do you really think I'm pretty?" the woman persisted, her fingers playing at the edges of the mask. They looked at each other, giggling. Then the spokesman for the three, with the bucket of eels in his arms said,

"Of course! You are pretty!"

In a swift, desperate motion, the woman tore the mask away, revealing a hideous, lipless triangular hole. Her teeth and gums stood out, sore-looking and unprotected.

"NOW DO YOU THINK I'M PRETTY?" she shrieked, and her voice was a searing wind that scattered the children, the eels flopping about on the cracked asphalt.

3

I dreamed about her after the broadcast, and in the dream she had a flawless face and lustrous eyes. She was contained in a sad mysterious light of her own making. It was the glimmer about her that seemed to cry out or resonate. She walked through a rich landscape while surrounded by a deep blue emptiness. She opened a bright janome umbrella and rain screamed to the ground.

On the day after the kite festival at the Nakatajima Dunes, it rained. In spite of the rain, it was very hot, and the whole school rang with an exquisite dread. Tokiwa Mabuchi was expelled on that day, before an audience of the entire student body in the gym. The big sliding doors had been opened to let in the damp air off the red-dirt tennis courts.

On a normal day at that hour, we would have seen Sister White, the young and bespectacled infirmary nun, dressed in her full white habit with the red cross embroidered across her breast, leading the tennis club exercises. Instead, all 1500 of us were arranged in long perfect rows, folded on the floor like a garden of black and silent flowers in a hothouse.

Along the side in folding chairs sat the nuns, with only their faces uncovered. Sister White had set free the expression on her face so that it was nowhere to be seen. She was the only one prepared to be bruised by the crisis.

Then Ishikawa-Sensei climbed upon the stage. He positioned himself in a stance of supreme ugliness beneath the heavy flags. He ordered Tokiwa to rise, and she found herself the only one standing.

The rain had stopped, and the light changed. Tokiwa had not lost her composure, and from where I sat I could clearly see her profile without turning my head. I felt the collective shudder that passed like an electric current through the big room, and glancing at Tokiwa I thought I saw her despair leaving her and flying into the rafters. Then the disciplinarian raised his finger and began his rapt and scathing expulsion.

The kite festival, with the bright and pretty lanterns twinkling all over the Nakatajima Dunes, had drawn her like a lightning bug. She wore a long magenta kimono and lipstick. She had put some glitter around her eyes and gone with some older boys, holding sweating bottles of iced sake. One of the boys had a fighting kite, and they watched him prepare its string with glass shavings.

I forget the details now of how she was caught.

"Everybody knows," shouted Ishikawa-Sensei,

"that the Nakatajima kite festival was OFF LIMITS. Except Sunday and in uniform. And everybody knows that only prostitutes wear makeup and cavort with men. But there are girls who are lower in both morals and intelligence than a dog. Just such a girl is there!"

His finger shot out. His mouth was a hideous little closed hole.

"Understand this clearly. This entire school is now shamed. To protect the rest of you, the enrollment of Tokiwa Mabuchi is terminated, effective immediately. And since no university can possibly accept her after being expelled from such a prestigious institution as this, she has by her actions of Saturday night, effectively ruined her future. Let her downfall serve as an example to anyone here who might even consider doing as she has done."

Tokiwa stood with her fingers laced before her. Tears streamed down her cheeks, and when they fell, they made a tapping sound on the floor. From the corner of my eye, I could see Mie Takayanagi's angry face. If I could have jumped up and drunk the tears from Tokiwa's cheeks I would have. I stole a glance at Mie, and she spread her fingers like a fan over her eyes. All at once the rain started again, as if it had only quietened itself in order to listen to what was taking place in the gym.

In my imagination I followed Tokiwa down the winding road, along the stone wall. I said to her,

"It doesn't matter. You did nothing wrong!"

But she had disappeared, and I could not find her anywhere.

Mie's mood was funereal as we walked the long distance to her house. We passed several vending machines selling iced coffee, and I became aware of how thirsty I was, but I did not have any money. As we passed through the shopping district, illuminated and vibrant, Mie said,

"I feel awful. That could have easily been me in Tokiwa's place."

"But you did not go to the Nakatajima Dunes," I said.

"I do other bad things. And so do you. And listen here, just because you come from America doesn't mean you can't get expelled."

We entered Mie's house through the bar at the front. It was a very old fashioned style sake bar, dark and wooden, with a distinctive, lush smell. Her father sat as always with a newspaper open in his lap and a cigarette between his lips. He barely acknowledged us when we entered. With his little cup and decanter before him sat the archery teacher on a mat. Mie paid

7

him no mind at all and filled a rice bowl full of sake. Then we went to her room. She opened the window and we each lit a cigarette. The archery teacher would never see us, no matter what we did right before his eyes. He wouldn't see because he didn't have to pay Mie's father.

Mie was in my class. She had looked so furious and was so oblivious to me that I had immediately liked her. I arrived in Japan with only one bag and the little case containing my rosary beads and a card reading: I am a Catholic. In case of an accident, please call a priest. Suddenly I was the only gaijin and one of the few real Catholics at this big, white-washed Catholic girls' school. Although I didn't count as an absolute gaijin, because of my dead Japanese-American Grampa, I was still surrounded at first by uninteresting, radish-legged girls who wanted to be my friend and speak English at me. I joined the kendo club, and during the day I followed Mie around. Then one day Sister Kawaguchi, the nun who carried a plastic ball-point with her name taped to it, took me by the arm. She dug her fingers into my skin out in the hall, with the rest of my class all pretending not to see.

"Takayanagi-San is a terrible student," she said. "You mustn't spend so much time with her. Why don't you make friends with some of the girls in the English Club?"

"I already speak English," I told her.

Sister Kawaguchi looked at me for a long moment, and I tried to appear sincere.

"Well then, the flower arranging club perhaps."

After school, in the shoe-room, Mie came to me. It was the first time she had ever approached me.

"What was Sister Kawaguchi talking to you about before?"

"She told me that you are not a good person to be friends with. She said that you are a terrible student, and I should be friends with the girls from the English Club."

Mie smiled.

"And you said what?"

"I said I already speak English."

Mie laughed out loud, her eyes bright. She reached out and slapped my head. She laughed some more, as she put on her big shoes, and then turned and slapped me again. That was how we became friends. Mie couldn't have cared less about English, but she corrected my Japanese. She also spoke at a normal speed with me, and I appreciated the normalcy she allowed me to feel. In no time, because I was

9

still a child, I could talk like everybody else.

We went out into the bar for more sake. The television was on, and we stood and watched the account of the cutmouth lady. The story eclipsed the expulsion, and we sat on the mat beside the archery teacher for a moment. He looked at the TV with disinterest. He was pale, slight, bald, and unmarried. He was a wordless and relentlessly ridiculed man. He had twitches in his face, but he was an excellent archer. We would watch him in his stance out behind the gym, the arrow pulled back to the limit, one eye open and the other closed. Whoosh.

In the evenings he'd come down to the Takayanagi sake bar and sit with his decanter and his ashtray until dark, and then get on his bike and ride tenuously off into the night.

My official guardian was a friend of an acquaintance of my mother. She owned a little noodle shop, but the customers really came to drink. She was called Mama, like all owners of places just like hers. I slept in a tiny, four-tatami room upstairs, next to another, slightly larger room where men played mah-jong. Sometimes they came drunkenly into my room, but always bowed out as soon as they realized their mistake. One of Mama's regulars was a beautiful girl called Akemi. Akemi was a student in Tokyo. She liked reggae and Mick Jagger, and her voice was husky and thick.

"You ought to come up and see me in Tokyo," she'd say to me, lighting a cigarette. "I'll take you to some great concerts."

One day she brought her younger brother in to meet me. He was called Ryutaro, and he wore eyeliner and went to the worst school in town.

"Why don't you two look out for each other," Akemi said.

Ryutaro and I had nowhere private to go. There was the underground coffee bar Akemi showed us and there were the stone steps of Hamamatsu Castle. Ryutaro wore his school uniforms baggy with the sleeves rolled up to his elbows. He looked so much like his older sister, and even wore her clothes sometimes. On the steps of the castle at night we could hear the elephants in the shadows of the zoo. We could look down on the neon glimmer of the city, surrounded on the steps by other couples who knew how to not see anybody else. Ryutaro was a terrible kisser, and when he reached into my starched white shirt, his hands were rough and inexperienced.

Akemi, Akemi, I thought, looking at his lips just like hers.

I was sitting in a cafe called Jusango Soko on the outskirts of town where no one I knew was likely to come. This cafe had good magazines and would serve me whiskey and water. They did not pay me any special attention.

I sat at a table in the darkest part of the room, in a dome of illumination from a little candle in a jar. When my whiskey came I read the first chapter of a serial comic in a ladies' magazine.

Yoko-san, a pretty, suffocating housewife, was the main character. She had the big liquid eyes and long limbs of most Japanese comic-book ladies.

Yoko-san was married to a salaryman. Most nights he stayed out late and came home drunk, and she would have to bring him dinner. A closeup drawing showed her husband passed out on the tatami. Yoko, wearing an angry expression, was drawn in at the kitchen sink.

During the daytime, Yoko did the marketing and the laundry. When she was young, she had wanted to be an artist. A sculptor, specifically. But then her arranged marriage had been agreed upon. Now when she saw young couples laughing together in the coffee shops in town she felt terribly, terribly lonely.

Finally one evening while her husband sat

with his face in his rice bowl, Yoko burst into tears.

"What are you crying for?" her husband asked.

"Oh, nothing, the humidity, I guess."

"When are you going to have the fan repaired, anyway?" he snapped.

The following day, Yoko signed up for a pottery class. The other women in the class were also housewives. The teacher was called Azumi, and she would have been beautiful as a man or a woman. During the first lesson, Yoko could hardly take her eyes from Azumi's face. Her long eyelashes cast shadows over her cheeks; her strong, graceful fingers gathered the clay into magnificent vases and tea cups. Yoko found her heart beating faster, and an agonizing shyness crippled her as it had so long ago and not so long ago, in school. It was admiration, that was all, admiration, she told herself riding home on the commuter train.

For days I thought of Azumi. I imagined kissing her, in spite of how ridiculous that was. Azumi, after all, was a comicbook character. After school I had to go all the way back to Jusango Soko on the bus just to look at her again, at her big eyes filled at once with enchantment, commotion and suffering.

13

I could hardly wait for the next issue, and when it finally came, my hands trembled as I opened the pages, sitting at my dark place in the corner.

There sat the ladies at their potters' wheels. After the class Yoko went to the market to buy food. On her way home she stopped into a tea shop. With the tea before her, Yoko looked up and found herself face to face with Azumi. Half of the next page was filled with only the blazing eyes and darkened cheeks of Yoko-san. She took in a gasp of air and stammered:

"Azumi-Sensei...Good Afternoon!"

"Why, Mrs. Morikawa, what a pleasant surprise to find you here."

"Oh, please, just call me Yoko, please."

"Allright, Yoko-san. May I join you for tea?"

Before too long the pottery teacher and her student were laughing together like best friends, as the afternoon turned inevitably to twilight. When they left the tea shop it was dark. They walked along together, side by side. The full enormous moon filled the sky, and big crows were drawn in glossy ink onto the sign at the end of the lane. STOP the sign said.

"When I was a young girl, in elementary

school, I had a good friend who was also called Yoko."

"Really?"

Yoko's heart began to race.

"Yes. We would walk each other home many times in one evening. She would walk with me to my doorway, and then we would turn around and walk back to her house. We hated to say goodbye."

"What ever happened to her?" Yoko asked.

"She—she DIED."

Here there was a closeup of Yoko's hand on Azumi's sleeve.

"I'm sorry, Azumi-Sensei."

The teacher left Yoko in front of her house and disappeared into the long shadows fallen across the street.

Yoko's husband was home, and he had three drunk salarymen with him.

"WHERE HAVE YOU BEEN?" he shouted. "My friends are here! I had to go into the kitchen, and I don't know where anything is!"

"I'm sorry, husband," Yoko said, looking at the floor. "Sit down, and I will bring you some-thing to eat."

She went into the kitchen, discovering a disaster of dirty dishes and empty bottles.

"What am I feeling, what am I feeling?" she asked herself, as she tied on her apron.

The image of Azumi's moist, terrifying eyes floated up above her.

The next week, when I climbed the narrow stairway to Jusango Soko, I was horrified to see through the window a woman just sitting down with the new issue of my magazine.

I went to my usual dark corner of the cafe and ordered a whiskey and water. The woman with the magazine had it opened to an article about Nobuko, the comedienne who had been caught smoking marijuana. I could see the picture, taken from her televised public apology. In the photo Nobuko was crying, and one of her false eyelashes had slid partway down her cheek and clung there.

I sat with my whiskey and waited. I certainly couldn't wait all night. The woman turned a page of the magazine every ten minutes. Finally, when I had worked myself into complete agitation, I got up, paid and went out. I walked quickly through the wet streets, past the video parlors and peepshow bars. Yakuza men with big hair stood outside the bars under the little awnings calling out to men passing by. I went into the Sanbancho Hotel and bought the magazine and a pack of Hope cigarettes.

When I got back to my little room, I sat on the tatami and opened the magazine.

Most of the women in the pottery class were plump and plain, but there were several who were pretty. Yoko carried her new vase to the kiln. Out of the corner of her eye, she watched Azumi-Sensei talking to one of the prettiest ones.

A stricken look came over her face. Leaving her vase on the workbench next to the kiln, she quietly slipped from the room. She bolted down the hall for the exit, while back in the classroom, Azumi-Sensei sat down to her mound of clay on the wheel.

Yoko ran through the streets until she found herself in front of SEIBU department store. Habit carried her toward the basement food-mart, but suddenly she jumped into the elevator and rode to the rooftop amusement park instead. She went to the Pound the Beaver game and dropped in a coin, grasping the mallet in her hand. The little fiberglass heads began popping up from their holes, and Yoko slammed them down madly.

In the evening, when Yoko's husband did not come home, she sat at the low table, watching the Drifters on TV and smoking. She poured herself a little glass of Suntory whiskey and the doorbell rang.

-Who could that be?, she thought, getting up and going to the door.

She opened it and drew in a sharp breath of air.

"Azumi-Sensei!"

"I hope I'm not disturbing you," Azumi-Sensei said. She had on a shiny leather jacket, and her big comicbook eyes glittered. In her long, elegant fingers she held a box.

"I wanted to bring you your vase. I fired it, and it is too beautiful to keep until next week."

They sat down at the table, and Yoko turned off the television.

"Would you like tea?" she offered.

"I'd much prefer a whiskey," Azumi said, gesturing at the bottle.

"Oh! Of course!" Yoko said, blushing very deeply, "Sometimes I like to have a little whiskey."

They sat looking at each other in the tiny room. Yoko looked away.

"Yoko-san..." Azumi-Sensei touched her hand. "I was worried about you; you left so abruptly. May I ask why?"

"But Azumi...Sensei...I think you know why!"

Yoko began to cry. She put her face into her hands with the beautiful creature, Azumi, watching. Azumi reached out her hand, and the page was filled with exploding stars.

"Yoko," she said, and then she kissed her. The kiss filled half the next page. They fell onto the tatami, and Azumi lay upon Yoko, whose hand, in the final drawing, grasped a leg of the low table.

After school I went with Mie to her house. We took the bus, with its velvet seats and wooden floorboards. On the bus I noticed a woman wearing a surgical mask. She had on a flowered dress and wore a thin gold watch on her wrist. She was frail but not unattractive. I quickly looked to her shoes, plain dark blue pumps, which matched her dark blue handbag. This could not have been the cutmouth lady. She was not elegant the way I imagined the cutmouth lady would have been. I lost interest and looked out the window as we passed an old wooden temple with carved stone foxes and then McDonald's.

We went through the sake bar where Mie's father sat on his stool smoking. He nodded to us. Mie went to the barrel to fill a bowl, and we went to her room. Her room was tiny, and she had none of the stuffed creatures on her narrow bed that lots of other girls had. But she did have a collection of antique hypodermic needles in a little glass case on a shelf, and the complete translated works of Edgar Allen Poe.

"Listen to this letter," she said to me, and pulled from her bed a copy of Olive Oil magazine, one of the many many magazines published for teenage girls.

Dear Miss Trouble,

I have been doing it to myself with a carrot for a long time. Then I tried it with a banana, and the banana broke off inside of me! I tried to get it out and I couldn't so I left it there and now it is starting to smell very bad, and I also have some pains too! From Yumi in Chiba

Mie closed the magazine and laughed.

"I don't believe that is a real letter," she said scornfully. "No girl is stupid enough to do something like that."

"Well, then, who do you think wrote it?"

"I think some stupid guy wrote it. Listen, how much have you and Ryu-chan done, anyway?"

She looked at me with something like disinterest.

"Hardly anything at all. We have nowhere to go. You know that."

It was the forbidden status of having a boyfriend that impressed Mie, and nothing more. In the same way she was impressed with my thinner than thin leather school satchel. We were all issued identical bags, black leather with two buckles and a handle. The thinner the bag the cooler it was, implying that there was nothing inside. Only radish-legged girls who joined the English club had fat ones. The best way to make the satchel thin was to immerse it in hot bathwater, then pile heavy books on it until it dried. I was lucky, though, because when I got mine, before I even knew the difference, I brought it into Mama's shop and sat with it at the counter.

Okei-chan the prostitute came in and sat down. When she saw my satchel, she started to laugh. Her gold teeth sparkled and she said,

"Darling, we need to do something about that!"

The next night she came in, wearing pink hot-pants, and gave me the bag she herself had used in school. It was a study in beauty, flat and supple, with a faded decal of Doraemon the blue spacecat still on its back.

One day, in the shoe-room, I left the bag propped against the wall while I changed from my indoor shoes to my outdoor shoes. Along came Sister Kawaguchi with her pen.

"Whose bag is this?" she demanded in her high, thin voice.

"It's mine, Sister," I said.

Everyone in the room, including Mie, tried not to laugh.

I stood behind Sister Kawaguchi, and from there I could see my skinny bag magnified in her bifocals. She shook her head and her wimple shivered.

"Where did you get this bag?" she asked sharply.

"It was from a friend of my mother," I lied.

"I see. Well, this is not a very nice one, and you will have to get a better one soon. This one won't even hold textbooks."

"Yes, Sister," I said.

But I did keep the bag, and years later, in the hidden inside pocket, I discovered a snapshot of Okei-chan, wearing the school sailor-uniform and smiling, long before she was a prostitute.

And all at once everyone at school was whispering cutmouth lady. All of the younger brothers and sisters had now "seen" her on their way to and from school. I myself saw her too, on the bus, quite often. But more often I dreamed about her, and in the dream she walked toward me, under a silver sky ready to rain. She held her hand over the surgical mask, and a little incandescent lightning bug followed behind her, illuminating her glossy hair.

"*I* think you're pretty!" I called out, across the water, from my place in the curve of the lane, "Akemi! Akemi!"

As we walked along, I told Mie about the serial comic. She listened with intense interest, and together we went to Jusango Soko so that she could look at the last issue. After she read it, in my dark corner place, we went out and walked along past the Shiseido Cosmetics plant and the parking garage with its giant neon letter P glowing over the street.

"Have you ever kissed a girl?" Mie asked me.

This question startled me, and I said,

"What do you mean exactly?"

"You know, like with Ryutaro, only a girl."

Mie's interest seemed scientific.

"Well, I've never really thought about it," I said. My voice was like a tin can falling down a well. I went on swiftly.

"What do you think about it, I mean, two girls kissing?"

Mie thought for a minute, her brow furrowed. While she was thinking I imagined what it might be like to kiss her, if she would let me, to see what it was like.

"I think," Mie said, "that it might be kind of pretty."

My imagination sped forward, and the idea of kissing Mie, my friend, seemed ludicrous but not impossible. I felt a small stab of panic, wondering if she had sensed what I was thinking.

"Well," I said, "what would you think if I told you that I had done it?"

"I would think that was sickening," Mie snapped.

"Well, don't worry," I said quickly, "I haven't."

"I wasn't worried."

"But if you were," I said.

The issue that followed almost steamed when I opened it. Azumi had brought Yoko to her house on the sea. Clearly she somehow had quite a lot of money. They had graphic cartoon sex on the terrace, with a gorgeous drawing of Azumi's face, biting her lip with her eyes squeezed shut, and then they did it again on Azumi's sleek sailboat.

Yoko had never in her life felt such bliss. At night, she watched Azumi sleep, while back at her tiny cinderblock apartment in the suburb of her unnamed city, her salaryman cursed her, pacing back and forth in the kitchen, calling for his midnight supper.

Azumi arranged to take the pottery class on a field trip. They would all travel to a tiny mountain village where there lived a famous potter. He had agreed to let the ladies observe him at work, Azumi told them, and this was a wonderful honor. They would stay at an old and distinguished inn and would be able to enjoy the nearby hotsprings.

They met at the train station, and while they waited on the platform for the shinkansen, Yoko tried to catch Azumi's eye. Azumi was busy talking with one of the older women in the class, and Yoko could hear her saying,

"I think that you especially will recognize the simple beauty of his craft, Mrs. Hisatomi."

Yoko boarded the train hopefully. Of course, Azumi-Sensei could hardly let on what was happening between them; this Yoko fully understood. She watched Azumi-Sensei sit down beside Mrs. Hisatomi several seats ahead and frowned in annoyance. Well at least, she considered, Azumi wasn't sitting beside Mrs. Momoi, who was young and beautiful and stylish. Mrs. Hisatomi was not young and had probably never been pretty. So Yoko relaxed and read a magazine.

Once at the inn, where they were to be four to a room, except for the teacher, of course, the ladies abandoned their luggage, and the entire class went to a restaurant to have dinner.

There were old women in the streets carrying big wire cages full of tiny, delicate red and yellow birds. Holy women dressed in red and white wraps clattered by wearing lacquered geta. On the way to have dinner, Azumi-Sensei looked at Yoko and smiled. Yoko understood this to be a special message, an invitation. Her heart beat wildly in her breast, and the sound of it, boom boom boom, was splashed across her chest in blue ink.

Much later, when all the lights had been extinguished and moonlight spilled into the room, Yoko listened to her sleeping roommates. All of them were older, and all of them were snoring.

Wrapped in her blue and white kimono stamped with the legend of the famous inn, she slid the shoji screen back and slipped out into the corridor. She crept along the wooden floorboards to Azumi's room. A smile came flying to her face, and she paused for a moment, listening. Then she quietly slid the door open just a crack. A single candle brought the room to glowing visibility, and Yoko clapped her hand over her mouth.

Inside, on Azumi's futon, over Yoko's shoulder, I could see the top halves of Azumi-Sensei and Mrs. Momoi in a taut embrace. My heart went cold, and Yoko slid the door silently closed. Then she stared out from the page, drawn all in green, her eyes brimming with tears.

One Saturday, after school which went till noon, I went to the underground cafe to meet Ryutaro. He was there when I arrived, hunched up over a POPEYE magazine. He had a cigarette between two fingers and tapped his black penny-loafer nervously. I sat down opposite him. He smiled at me. "OH!" he said, his usual greeting. I ordered an iced coffee, and Ryutaro stared at his magazine.

"Look, why are you acting so weird?" I asked him.

He sighed and closed his magazine. He rolled his eyes to the ceiling. I noticed a different shade of eyeliner, and he had added eye *shadow* now as well.

"OK, I guess I really have to tell you," he said, sighing again.

"What," I said, "What?"

Ryutaro leaned towards me, and his forehead wrinkled up the way Akemi's did.

"The reason I'm telling you this," he said, "is because I don't want you to hear it from somebody at your school first. And let me say beforehand that it didn't mean a thing to me."

Now I felt a pang of disquietude, but I said nothing.

"I was at a party last night. And we all got drunk, and I made it with a girl who goes to your school."

"Oh," I said. Then the waiter brought my iced coffee and placed it on a little black paper doily.

"Listen, it didn't mean a thing. For one thing, I was completely drunk, and for another, she's ugly. She's made it with a lot of guys I know. She's cheap. She's even done it with girls."

"She's what!" I almost shouted.

Ryutaro began to laugh sympathetically. He must have thought I was horrified and shocked or worse.

"Haven't you ever heard of that?" He asked me, the smile still on his lips. "Girls and girls. Some of them are like that."

"What is this girl's name?" I demanded.

For a moment he looked worried.

"You won't make a scene or anything, will you?"

"I think I have the right to know who it was, since I'm sure she knows who I am," I said angrily.

Ryutaro looked embarrassed. He knew as well as I did that I was as much a status symbol for him as he was for me. Having a gaijin girlfriend couldn't have hurt his reputation any with his baggy suited friends.

"OK," he said. "Her name is Kaori, and she's in the second year Orchid class."

I didn't know her name. But when I went to the third floor and waited outside of the Orchid classroom on the next Monday, I immediately knew who Kaori was. She looked right at me, wearing a mocking smile, when she came out. I had seen her around in the hallways, this girl, with her acne and big round face and small, mean eyes. She was one of the glue-sniffers, that much I knew about her. But now she held for me a special interest. She approached me, still wearing the smile.

"So?" she said.

"So you saw Ryu-chan the other night." I deliberately added the affectionate tag to his name.

"Oh, he told you?"

"Of course he told me," I said. "He gets drunk now and then. So what?"

"Right," said Kaori. "So what."

She started to walk away and join her friends, a little circle of creepy girls who waited for her languidly at the end of the hall.

"Wait," I said, and she turned around.

"Can I come to your house sometime?" I almost whispered.

She cocked her head to one side, surprised, and said,

"How much money do you have?"

"Oh, about 1000 yen."

"Why don't you come Wednesday night, then?" she said quietly.

"You do understand what I mean, don't you?"

Kaori nodded. "Of course I do," she said, and then, after giving me directions to her house, she was gone.

I stood still in the hallway for a few minutes. What had I just done, I asked myself. I pictured the neighborhood she lived in, rundown and dreary, near the railway station and the factories. It was where a muddy wasteland began, stretching out to meet the Uni discount shopping center and the grey cinderblock apartment towers numbered one through infinity. Sister Kawaguchi appeared at the end of the hallway.

"And what are you doing up on this floor?" she said, taking my elbow into her tight grip. "This is not your floor, and you should be getting changed for afterschool clean-up, should you not?"

In the evening the TV reported another official encounter with the Cutmouth Lady.

A child eight or nine years old was on her way home from school in the late afternoon. She stopped in the center of a stone bridge, to look down on a group of long legged birds who had a nest on the bank of the canal, of which they were fiercely defensive. A very elegant woman, classically dressed in a Spring yukata and wooden geta and wearing a surgical mask, stopped beside her.

"Aren't they lovely?" the woman asked.

The child glanced at her and nodded. She was a shy child and kept her eyes averted. The woman took a few small, clattery steps away. Then turning back, with her fingers trembling about the edges of her mask, she asked,

"Do you think I'm lovely?"

She doubled over to look the little girl squarely in the face, then reached out to take her chin between two fingers.

"Do you?" she asked again.

The little girl answered yes. Then in a flurry of dark cotton the mask was torn away, its ghastly secret uncovered.

"Do you *really* find me lovely?" hissed the sepulchral mouth, the eyes above it narrowed to slits.

The child opened her mouth to scream, she tried to make her legs run, but instead she fainted onto the flagstones of the bridge. While she lay unconscious, the cutmouth lady smeared rose-red lipstick onto her little mouth.

The TV announcer finished up by saying that the child, whose name was Sachiko and who liked origami and Doraemon the cat, was being treated for shock and would miss some days of school. Otherwise, she was unharmed.

For several days the media buzzed over the

woman in the mask. What was she, a ghost from an antique horror story come to life? More than likely, it was decided, she was a victim of a botched surgery or an accident gone insane. She was to be pitied, but now she had touched a child, and there was no telling to what degree her misery would escalate.

I sat in a dark corner of Jusango Soko with the magazine. Poor Yoko lay on the bed in her cinderblock apartment. She was wracked with a pain almost physical, imagining over and over Azumi-Sensei in an ecstatic swoon with Mrs. Momoi. She left her body inert upon the bed and swam into a dark, roiling world of grief and poison. She found herself encircled by a long black death adder of jealousy, a sigh of agony issuing forth from its wide open, fang-glistening mouth.

"NO, NO, NO!" she cried out, and flung the empty whiskey bottle at the grey painted bricks. The bottle exploded, sending a shower of silver slivers and shards over the room. The noise brought Yoko momentarily to her senses. The light outside was waning and soon night would come. Her husband might come home, and she couldn't let herself be seen like this. All day long the phone had been ringing and she had been ignoring it. It could only have been Azumi. Her husband never called, and she had no friends. So she let it ring and ring, imagining herself explaining by saying, "I was ill, ill, ill."

She went to the closet for the broom and dustpan and swept up the pieces of glass. As she was bending to empty the dustpan into the trash, an idea took form in her head. She emptied the glass instead into a paper bag, which she then wrapped in a cloth and put into her handbag.

Her husband came home earlier than usual, and Yoko prepared Katsudon, then sat nearby while he ate to replenish his beer before he had to ask. The next morning, she went very early to the pottery classroom. The building was deserted, but even so, Yoko took care that nobody saw her enter. The room was still and silent, its big canvas curtains hanging over the windows. The worktables were all empty, and only the teacher's area was prepared. The mound of clay sat on the wheel, ready to be formed into something delicate and lovely, and Yoko went to it, opening her handbag. She pulled out the cloth and took out the paper bag. Carefully, as if she were performing a surgery, she slid the longest, sharpest slices of the glass one by one into the supple clay. She counted the pieces as they went in, until she had inserted forty. Then, with great delicacy, she smoothed the surface of the mound so that it concealed with absolute discretion its secret enhancement.

"You will never," murmured Yoko to herself, "make love with those beautiful hands again!"

All during that Wednesday I tried to avoid Mie. I dreamed my way through Sister Kawaguchi's geography lesson, thinking of the horrifying sight it must have been, watching the man who drank the coca cola in the phone booth. One of the newspapers said that he had clawed the pavement until his fingers split and bled. Then I was pulled to the present by the sister's black pen rapping against my desk. She looked at me, imploring me to pay attention for just once. Mie stared at me from across the room, frowning when I ignored her.

After school she chased me as I tried to steal out the front gates instead of the usual way out back.

"What's with you?" she said. "Where are you sneaking off to like a little snake?"

"I have things to do at home," I told her, and then I said goodbye and got on the bus. I went home and changed into blue jeans and a sweatshirt. I folded a 1000 yen note and slipped it into my back pocket. Then I went out. I went to the underground cafe to wait

35

until dusk, half hoping that Ryutaro would be there. I sat and looked at magazines until 8:30. Then I paid and walked to the railway station. It was not difficult to find the little street Kaori had described to me, a street lined with archaic, run-down houses made of wood and paper, houses built before the war, with no indoor plumbing.

Kaori's was the fourth house in from the main road, set back behind a single, twisted pine tree. She did not live with her parents, for reasons I never knew; maybe her parents were dead or didn't want her. In any case, she lived in a room in this antique wood and paper house with two very old women who were somehow related to each other.

I rang the little bell outside the door and waited. The house was dark and still, and for a moment I wondered if a trick were being played upon me. I started to feel very nervous and cold. Then the door opened, and a tiny, ancient woman stood before me, holding a flickering lantern. She looked to be in her nineties and was so completely bent over from years spent in the rice fields that she had to twist her neck in order to look up at me. She wore a dark kimono and said nothing when I told her I was there to call on Kaori. She stepped aside, and I carefully removed my shoes and went in. She led me down a long, narrow hall, at the end of which I could see the blue shimmer of a television. The old woman, who still had not said a word, stopped in front of a doorway and pointed. Then she continued down the hallway in her bent, labored shuffle, and disappeared.

I tapped on the door. I felt suddenly miserable as the door opened and I came face to face with Kaori on the other side. She invited me in. Her room was strewn with dirty clothes and magazines, empty cigarette packs crumpled here and there, and full ashtrays sitting all over the floor. Kaori told me to sit down. She lit a cigarette and offered me one.

"So," she said, "when did you have your first kiss?"

I stammered. I said something, made something up, I suppose, not wanting to give anything truthful about myself to Kaori. I looked at her big, acne covered face, her sneer of a smile. Akemi, I thought to myself. And even drunk, how could Ryutaro have beared to kiss this girl? Still, it was my chance to know how it was done, so I thought of Azumi, trying to warm myself toward my opportunity.

Kaori puffed on her cigarette.

"What's it like being foreign, anyway?" she asked. "Is the hair on your pussy the same color as the hair on your head?"

37

She burst out laughing and opening a big brown bottle of sake, she took a long pull on it and offered it to me. I shook my head. She set the bottle down and started unbuttoning her blouse. She still had on her school uniform, and she quickly unzipped the jumper and stepped out of it. She took off the blouse and unhooked her bra. Her large breasts spilled out, and turning to me, she took one in her hand.

"You can kiss it, if you want to," she said.

I felt ill, as if I were going to faint. I didn't want this to be the way I would always remember it, and when she knelt down in front of me, I caught the sharp-sweet smell of her skin and the sake on her breath. She touched her lips to mine wetly, and I pushed her away and stood up.

"What do you think you're doing?" I said to her, backing toward the doorway. I turned and went quickly out. I rushed down the hall and out into the humid air, where I didn't stop to put on my shoes, but picked them up and ran barefoot into the street. I was momentarily disoriented and turned the wrong way. I stopped to shove my feet into my shoes, then found myself at a dead-end. I had to turn and go back, and when I passed her house, Kaori was standing out in front, laughing and shaking her head.

For a long time I wandered around the city feeling as if I had been flayed. I finally ended up going to Mie's. I told her what had happened. She listened and then she laughed at me and slapped my head.

"If you only wanted to kiss a girl," she said, "I would have kissed you myself for 1000 yen! You are an idiot, such an idiot."

I worried about what Kaori might tell everyone, but it was just as Mie promised: no one would have believed that I would have offered money to have sex with someone like her; it would only have made her look stupid to tell anyone. And if she did, it did not come back to me.

I didn't see much of Ryutaro after that, but it didn't matter. I went to Jusango Soko to see Azumi in the hospital, with both hands wrapped in white gauze bandages. She looked terribly sad. She really didn't deserve it, I thought at Yoko, who sat in the asylum smiling.

I remember the day they arrested the man with the icepick on the train, and he turned out to be a sushi maker. I saw people across the train tracks talking about it, tapping two fingers into their palms, the way sushi makers work. They never caught the poisoner but guessed that he worked in a chemical plant because of the industrial poison found all throughout the bodies of the victims. And nobody ever knew who the cutmouth lady really was, or if they did, I never heard about it. After awhile there were so many sightings all over Japan, from Kyushu to Hokkaido, that no one bothered to believe it anymore, and maybe she was a ghost from an antique horror story.

Just before the summer holiday I went to have a cholera vaccination. After the shot I felt giddy and faint, walking through the pleasure district in the hot sun. I stopped for an iced tea in a little cafe, and while I sat inside I thought I saw Tokiwa Mabuchi walking past outside. I quickly paid my bill and ran out after her, but if it had been her she was swallowed up into the crowd, and I couldn't see her anywhere.

IN A MOUNTAIN GARDEN
I DREAMED MYSELF SLEEPING

Mari Shimada was the girl in my class who burned her skin with me. One day during the cooking lesson, standing in a circle around the gas range, I caught her looking at me with her lidless eyes. The liquid wind from outside all but drowned Sister Sugiura's voice, and I glanced back at Mari Shimada. She had closed her eyes and faced the windows, where outside cherry blossoms were falling all over the wet ground and the rain hung its drops on the air as if all over a spider's web.

After the lesson she signaled for me to wait. When everyone had gone, and we watched Sister Sugiura disappear through the side door of the convent, Mari uncorked a big bottle of cooking sake and poured a bowlful.

"Drink it down!" she said, pushing it at me.

The wind brought a spray of rain in through the open window, and my skin prickled with a chill as I took the bowl in both hands and drank it fast, like water, spilling it over my chin. She took it from me and wiped my chin with her palm. Looking over her shoulder at the empty doorway, she quickly poured more sake and drank it herself. She looked me in the eye over the rim of the bowl, then she lowered it and smiled.

"I just wanted to see if you'd do it," she said, and I heard myself breathing as if I'd been running. I could still feel her palm against my chin.

"Listen," she said, rinsing the bowl in the sink, "the water going down the drain sounds like Middle Eastern singing." Later I saw Mari Shimada looking down at me from up in my dreams, and from then on I could no longer think of her without an ache in my chest.

Both of her parents were physicians, and they owned a private hospital. Their three-storied townhouse behind the hospital had its own roof garden and swimming pool.

I went to visit one Sunday in the rain, and rang the bell at the iron gate facing the street. An old woman wearing an apron over her dark kimono came out of the house, carrying an umbrella, and opened the gate for me. She took me into a tiled entryway where I removed my shoes and put on the slippers she offered. Then she led me into a large room on the ground floor. I sat on an enormous rose-colored sofa draped with the skin of a grizzly bear, its head resting on the floor.

There I waited until Mari Shimada entered the room silently and sat at the end of the sofa, wearing pink lipstick, and dressed in a black silk skirt and blouse. I could see a blue vein pulsing in her neck. The old woman came into the room with a tray of tea things and set it on the table, beside a bowl of pears.

"Would you like anything else?" she asked.

"No, thank you."

The old woman bowed her head and went out.

"Is that your grandma?" I asked her.

Mari Shimada laughed. "No," she said.

I followed her into a smaller, Japanese style sitting room, with tall windows looking onto a manicured rainy garden. She poured tea, sitting up on her knees beside me, and then she sat back and gazed out the window.

The emptiness of the big house rushed in my ears like the ocean in a seashell, and in the damp garden light I was able to see the loneliness all about her. It didn't matter that we didn't say anything. When she leaned over to pour more tea, I saw again the blue vein stand out against the translucent skin of her neck, and I almost loved her.

Early in the morning one day, there was an assembly called on the red dirt tennis courts. We were in long perfect identical rows of black and white. The Mother Superior climbed upon the platform and the disciplinarian's voice rang out. We turned to face the old Mother Superior who had advanced Parkinson's and shook like a rag on a clothes line.

"Good morning," she said into the microphone. Her voice came from the high speakers behind us, at the far end of the tennis courts.

"Good morning," we answered her.

"I would like to tell you students that I am very proud of all of you, and that I pray for you all to continue with the diligence and rigour which gives this school its proud name. But there have been several incidents, isolated ones I must add, which trouble me deeply. And that is why I have called this assembly today."

The Mother Superior pushed her glasses up and gazed out at us, her face shaking back and forth as if she were looking us over and saying, no, no, no, no, no.

"I cannot go into the depth of these indelicacies which have been brought to my attention; I can only stress that while friendships are a gift to us from God, and there is nothing more holy than true friendship, we must not let certain types of friends interfere with our studies. Remember, one jeopardy in a place such as this is a hazard to us all. I recommend that we enjoy our free time in groups of friends, rather than paired off and isolated. The strength is in the group, remember."

She opened her hymnal. Sister Kawaguchi climbed up onto the platform beside her carrying a tape recorder.

"We'll sing hymn number 128," the Mother Superior said, fidgeting with the mike. Sister Kawaguchi turned on the tape recorder and held it to the microphone, producing a shriek of feedback from the tall PA. A murmur rippled through the student body, and Sister Kawaguchi and the Mother Superior faced each other, bending over the tape recorder and shaking their heads. Then Sister Kawaguchi tried again. The air filled with tinny piano music, and the Mother Superior's voice began to quaver and then sing. We all followed along and two girls in front of me began to shake with barely stifled laughter.

The bad recording along with the Mother

Superior's fluttery singing was laughable, and
the laughter of the girls in front of me was con-
tagious. I tried to force off the capricious
demon but it swam all around me and I felt the
laugh welling up and spilling out of me. I
caught it in my hand but Mr. Cockroach the
disciplinarian was at that moment creeping
past and glimpsed me holding it. He wove himself into the black cornfield of us and hit me
on the neck with the sharp edge of his metal
yardstick. I bit into my lip as my aborted
laughter melted into a stifled cry.

The hymn ended, and Sister Kawaguchi
read from Leviticus, the weeping and gnashing
of teeth, while I dared not reach up to touch
the throbbing place on my neck from where a
warm wetness was now trickling.

When the assembly was finished, the clouds
had turned green-gray and threatening, and I
caught sight of Mari Shimada running across
the parking lot towards the main gate. I
squinted my eyes and watched her climb into a
white Austin Healy which sat waiting just outside the cast iron bars of the high gate. Then
the rain started to fall in big soaking drops and
everyone burst into a run for their shoe-rooms
in a noisy, chilly commotion.

During Sister Sugiura's cooking lesson the
room felt unbearably drab and I thought I

might scream out in boredom. Sister Sugiura was explaining how to bake a potato. All of the many, many ways that one can manipulate this wonderful fruit, she was saying, offer innumerable delightful tastes. In France, she explained, they call this the apple of the earth. And indeed, cutting into a raw potato, you can see that it is very much resembling an apple in texture, in look. But raw is one way that it is not good to eat a potato. And on this day, she told us, we were going to learn how to bake the potato, and then how to enhance it with Sister Mochizuki's hand-made butter and long green grasses from the garden behind the chapel.

The urgent way Mari Shimada had clutched at her side as she ran across the parking lot filled me with trepidation. There was an opening in the clouds through which a strange diluted sun was spilling, filling the austere classroom with melancholia.

I watched the quiet faces of my classmates, looking on as Sister Sugiura pulled a hot potato from the oven by the edges of its foil, burning her fingers and putting the tips of them into her mouth. In the sepia colored light from outside, I could imagine these faces in an old photograph. With the white enamel cookware, Sister Sugiura in her frameless spectacles placing the big black kettle over the circle of pointed blue and hissing gas jets like an eerie little choir, and the timeless faces of my classmates, it might have been a hundred years ago, I thought. Today is a memory preparing itself for when I am old, I thought to myself.

It did not take much wondering to find out that Dr. Shimada, her mother, was the one who drove the Healy. It was her mother who collected automobiles in the underground garage beneath the house. The Healy was her favorite one. Strangely, Dr. Shimada, her father, did not drive at all. He was frightened of it. Mari told me this and I laughed at first, thinking she was joking.

"All of these cars belong to your mother?"

Lined side by side, the Austin Healy, the old Mercedes sedan, a Citroen, a Jaguar and a Cedric.

Mari Shimada nodded her head. Her father, she said, was nakiyasui as well, quick to cry, over just about anything. Except medicine. Forget about going to him if you didn't feel well, she said. Noone could be less sympathetic than a parent who is a doctor. They see too many serious illnesses to worry about a stomach ache.

The invitations to her house became more frequent, and I often went there for dinner. We would eat in a large opulent drawing room full of western antiques and a gigantic bi-lingual television. There was a button to push whereby a dubbed foreign program could be heard in its original language. We were always served by old Mrs. Kakiuchi in her swishing dark linen kimono. Once, Dr. Shimada slid the door open and stepped in while we sat eating shabu shabu. She was a perfectly beautiful creature, much younger in appearance than she must have been, wearing her hair pulled back and almost no makeup. Glamorous and long-limbed. She had come to get a book she needed, she said, and she pulled the ladder on its track along the high wall of books at one end of the room. On her way out she turned and excused herself for having interrupted us.

Mari looked at the television, her chopsticks in her fist. Her face betrayed nothing. I guessed that she just knew her so well that she couldn't even see her.

"She's beautiful, you mother," I said.

"Really? She thinks she is beautiful, too," said Mari. "She's leaving for Monaco soon. She treats people there, she goes every four months and stays a month."

"You don't miss her when she's gone?"

She shrugged, still looking at the television. Kaori Momoi was on singing a song about the word busu, ugly girl, and where it came from. Busu, she sang, whoever could have thought up that word? Bu Su, just two little sounds, after all...

"In the summer holiday," Mari said, "I go too. We have an apartment there."

She got up and brought a big bottle of sake from a cabinet. She poured a clay bottle full and put it into the little microwave under the television. When I swallowed the hot sake, I felt a glow of excitement spread through me, like success, like majesty, Monaco. But it was only alcohol.

Mari Shimada's father never left Hamamatsu except to attend occasional medical conferences in Tokyo or Osaka. And then he took the shinkansen, not without a little fear. He had never flown in an airplane, so he never went to Monaco. It was her mother who was the specialist; she was an eye surgeon, and her father was more of a local general practitioner. It seemed that her mother never stopped moving. She would go to Italy just to buy a new Fendi bag, Mari told me, and she liked to attend auctions. She had priceless original oils wrapped in paper just sitting in her bedroom closets. She bought clothing worn by famous actresses in old movies and kept them in garment bags.

Mari took me upstairs to her mother's suite of rooms. She leaned in the doorway of one room, while I looked at the ornate marble hearth, a Kawai grand piano. She pointed to a doorway in the far wall and said, "That room is only clothes and bags." Dr. Shimada's bedroom was in another time, with a sleigh bed from France and a display case full of precious antique Venetian glass. Vases of cut flowers standing all over the floor under an open window. It was almost too much to take in.

"Even when she isn't here," Mari said, "my mother likes to have fresh flowers every day." She shrugged her shoulders. I felt as if this were a museum of which she were the curator. There were no personal effects lying about anywhere in these rooms, and I imagined a velvet rope strung across the doorways, and a tour-guide saying, this was where the famous so-and-so slept.

One evening, Mari and I were sitting on the tatami in the little garden room, when her father abruptly pushed his head through the door. He was a small, exhausted looking man with graying hair, wearing a white doctor's coat and a stethoscope around his neck. He had the same lidless eyes as Mari, and I caught the aroma of disinfectant as he looked quickly at me and nodded his head.

"Mari-chan," he said, "please come for a few minutes."

She got to her feet and went to the door without looking at me. Her father glanced my way and said,

"Please excuse us, it will only be a little moment." Then they went out and slid the door closed.

I found myself alone in the sparse, calm room, where in the garden a little cherry tree, standing alone close to the stone wall, appeared to be looking in at me. I poured more tea and lay back onto the tatami. After about ten minutes, Mari returned and sat down. She didn't say anything, but when she looked at me I felt like crying.

What sadness filled this marvelous house loaded with beautiful, expensive unnecessary objects. I looked into her face and she shook her head at me.

"What did he want?" I asked her.

"My father needs help with things, that's all. When my mother isn't here, especially. What a trap I feel myself caught in some-times."

There was a nightclub just opened which Mari wanted to go to. If she told her father she was staying with me, and I told my guardian that I was staying at the house of Drs. Shimada, we could go out. But we would have to slip into the hospital if we wanted to sleep. She had done it before, slept in an empty room of the hospital. If we tried to enter the house, her father would waken because he heard everything. He was lenient to a degree, she said, but not that far.

Mari lent me some beautiful clothes to wear on that night, and called a taxi. We went to a part of town I almost never visited, stopping in front of an illuminated building guarded by two men in white suits. We got out and the men opened the doors for us. We went in and a hostess in a leather jumpsuit leapt forward and took us by the arms, startling me and making Mari laugh. The hostess had leather cat's ears and heavy black khol all around her eyes. She didn't say anything but took us up the winding, black carpeted stairs to a room with a tiny bar and a few little tables.

As we sat down at one of the tables, I noticed that instead of walls there were large glass panes, behind which were tamo trees and raked gravel, and winding through the trees were delicate pathways and reproductions of bridges from around the world. The lighting inside this terrarium was subdued, but I could see little houses arranged in the branches of the trees, and before long I started to see the cats, sleek, supple cats, coming out of the houses and wandering about the pathways, crossing the bridges. I could not believe my eyes. I looked at Mari, who sat with her lips parted, the candle flame from the table fluttering in her widened eyes.

The hostess asked us what we would like, and Mari ordered a bottle of champagne. The hostess glided over to the bar and returned with a bottle decorated with flowers and an ice bucket. When she had poured the champagne, she went to a cabinet and put a tape in, and rich sound filled the room. "Those cats," Mari said to the hostess who had curled around her feet, "they are so content and relaxed."

The hostess smiled. "They can't see or hear us," she said, "the gardens are soundproof, and the glass to them is only a mirror. And they are very well fed and looked after."

Later the hostess took us up another flight of stairs to a ballroom, where there were people dancing on a wide wooden floor to Frank Sinatra, and waiters in white coats carried silver trays of drinks to the tables around its edges. We watched for awhile then followed our hostess to a room with another terrarium, but this one was a beautiful cemetery, where little monkeys with great wisps of long white hair swept back from their foreheads leapt in and out of soapstone mausoleums. This one was lit so as to create the illusion of infinite distance and the little trees in the foreground threw leafy shadows onto the chalky tombs.

We had another bottle of champagne in the monkey room, along with fresh shrimps and little oysters brought by our hostess. There was nothing at all in my head, so utterly captivating were the rooms and decorations of the bewitching place. Other guests floated in and out of our vision accompanied by their various hostesses, trailing cords of cigarette smoke behind them. It wasn't until we had finished three bottles of champagne and were ferried along on a current of high euphoria that Mari Shimada asked for the bill. She gave the hostess her credit card and then we stepped into the purring taxi waiting in front of the building.

I felt that only an hour or two had passed in the enchanted night club, but it was past five in the morning when the taxi let us off in front of Shimada Hospital. Mari motioned for me to follow her and we went around to the side where there was an emergency entrance.

We pushed the glass door open and entered the sterile hallway. Mari pulled off her shoes and put them in a plastic bag she'd concealed behind a fire extinguisher. Then she held the bag out for me. We went carefully down the polished tile floor, past rooms where an arm or a plastered leg could be seen hanging above a bed in the blue light of early morning. Mari turned and pressed a finger to her lips, and we turned a corner where at the end of another hallway, I could make out a nurse dozing behind a desk. We slipped into an empty room with a bare bed and Mari quietly closed the door.

We would have to slip out again between 7:30 and 8:00, when the nurses were changing shifts, she was whispering. But we could at least take a nap in the meantime. We lay down on the bare hospital bed, and Mari seemed to fall instantly asleep, while I lay beside her never more awake, listening to her careful breathing.

It was not long after that delirious night that I saw Dr. Shimada and his pale face again. After Saturday school, I went with Mari Shimada to her house, and she left me in the second floor library while she went to change her clothes. While she was gone I had to pee, so I went to look for the toilet. The second floor was somewhat of a maze of hallways and doors, and I went towards a door left ajar which looked like it might be the toilet.

I pushed the door soundlessly open and my breath caught in my throat. There was Dr. Shimada, his back to me, standing at a little wheeled table, with his sleeve rolled up and a rubber cord tightened around his forearm. He was pushing the plunger of a hypodermic needle, embedded deep in a blue vein which stood out almost obscenely.

He wasn't aware of my presence, and I stared as he pulled the needle out, expelling a long, rasping sigh. He lay the spent needle on the table and slowly untied the rubber cord. He rolled his sleeve back down. Then his shoulders began to gently shiver, and I heard the almost unearthly sound of Dr. Shimada sobbing. I backed up carefully, pulling the door to where it had been, and crept back to the library.

When Mari returned we went to the big drawing room to watch television. She sat beside me on the sofa and held my hand in her lap. The old woman ushered in two delivery men with a big crate.

"Just set it down over here," she said. She bent over and squinted at the packing label.

"Contents: Two antique roulette tables" she read slowly. "It's from Dr. Shimada from Monaco," she said, straightening. Mari rolled her eyes and looked sidelong at me.

"You see? Now she's having roulette tables air freighted from Europe. And she doesn't even know how to gamble."

In a dream I saw a foreign moon behind my eyes, a wild fire on a rolling hill. Dr. Shimada signaled the auctioneer in her doctor's coat and glasses, her teeth immense and gleaming. She ripped silver hypodermics from her arms and sailed them into a dart board decorated with a raven's head. I marveled at the cluster of needles bristling out from the red bull's eye, and Dr. Shimada swept a pile of banknotes off the table into her bag.

Sometime during the night, the Mother Superior had a stroke and was taken by helicopter to a Catholic Hospice in Nagoya. The Head Mistress called an assembly in the gymnasium. Rain poured down outside, and streaks of green lightning reached down and touched the ground. We sat quietly on our knees, and the nuns placed baskets of candles at the head of each row, passed hand by hand until everyone held one. Little Bic lighters followed, and the gymnasium glowed.

The Head Mistress climbed upon the stage under the school flag printed with the word Veritas and the white and red flag of Japan. She bowed her head and began to pray. "Heavenly Father, we humbly ask you to keep

gentle watch over our beloved Mother
Superior, to alleviate her suffering and return
her to this place upon where she is so depend-
ed and adored. We ask for strength and guid-
ance, and for understanding of what we need to
do in her absence to please her. In the name of
Christ, our Father, Amen." A hushed Amen
rose up from the rows of all of us.

She looked up and wiped her eyes with a
tissue. "Everyone," she said, "our Mother
Superior has had a very serious stroke, and
while I pray that she will recover and return to
us, she is very, very ill at the moment. Do not
forget her dedication to you all, that she came
here from France almost sixty years ago as a
young nun to found this school. Some of your
grandmothers, and many of your mothers and
aunts were here, and all of what they've taken
forth into their lives were given by Her. Please
pray for her well-being, and I might say, to the
many of you who are in fact non-Catholics,
prayer is prayer, and I ask it of you just the
same."

Along the far wall the nuns sat in chairs
facing the stage. Sister White the nurse had
taken off her glasses. I saw her face wet with
tears. Even Sister Kawaguchi was overcome,
and her chin trembled like a real person's.
I saw a bit of color in her hand as she wiped her
eyes with a hanky.

I had only spoken to the Mother Superior a few times, but she was a very kindly and gentle person. We were all children to her, and her eyes were soft when she looked at us, even when scolding. The third-year choir got up on the stage and sang Our Eyes Are Raised to Heaven. My throat ached as I rubbed my blood red rosary beads and listened to their elysian voices.

The following day the Mother Superior died, and the school closed for that day. I went to Mari Shimada's house. She looked terrible, her skin bluish and her hair mussed, and the red t -shirt she wore had a large, damp stain down the front of it. She took me into the downstairs kitchen where she was making tea.

"What's wrong, Mari-san," I asked her. "Is it the Mother Superior?"

She looked at me with a wry smile and shook her head.

"I've never even spoken to her," she said, "and I am not a Catholic, either."

She pulled out a chair and sat across from me at the table. Her brow furrowed and she rested her chin in the palm of her hand.

"Well then what is it? Are you sick?"

She sighed and closed her eyes. "No, I'm

not sick. My father had an emergency call, Mrs. Kakiuchi has the day off, and it has been difficult."

I looked around the big kitchen, at the black kettle on the sleek steel range, the cloud of steam rising out of it. What could be difficult here? Did she need Mrs. Kakiuchi even to make a cup of tea? I felt a pang of something like annoyance, but then I looked at the sad, beautiful face of Mari Shimada and my irritation faded as quickly as it had risen.

Mari poured tea, and then she sat down again. "I like you so much," she said almost bitterly, "that I sometimes think it's a tragedy. That one of us is the wrong sex. If only, if only, I think. If only I were a boy, things would be so different." Her hands shook as she took hold of her teacup. "How do you mean?" I asked her.

"Something good, something to look forward to, I don't know," she shook her head and leaned over the table with her forehead against the back of her hand.

"Do you give yourself injections like Dr. Shimada?" I heard myself ask, and she looked up at me abruptly, with wild eyes full of suffering.

"How do you know about him?"

For an instant I thought she might leap up

and slap me. "I—I saw him, upstairs one day, by accident. I didn't mean to see it!"

Mari pressed her hands to her head and moaned quietly.

"He's a morphine addict, my father. But no, I have never injected anything. That you could even wonder such a thing! My father, believe it or not, thinks that nobody knows he does it."

"Why does he?" I asked her. "Does your mother?"

Mari gave a little shout of laughter. "My mother? Most definitely not! She's hoisted that man into an ice-bath too many times to want any part of it herself. I told you, she buys things, she spends money, she flies around the globe so fast it spins. That is what she does. She can't face it, she can't. She is an eye surgeon. She lives for the picturesque."

Mari stood up and asked me to follow her. "I want you to know this," she said. We went up the stairs, then up the next flight, to the third floor where I had never been except in passing on the way to the roof garden. We went down the carpeted corridor and around a corner. At the end of that hallway was a door, slightly ajar.

"You will be the only one who knows," she

said to me, and she raised her brows ever so slightly. I was filled with apprehension, following her towards the door. She pushed it open and stepped inside. I was not prepared for what I saw.

Lying on a railed-in bed in a sweatsuit was a boy of about nineteen or twenty. He turned his head in our direction, and his mouth opened, issuing forth a high cry, like a whine. He flailed his arms and bucked like a wounded horse. But the horror was not his cries and movements. Where his eyes would have been, there was only skin, skin with indentions, like thumb prints in new bread. I felt my breath sucked away from me, and Mari took me by the arm.

"This is Hiroyuki, my older brother," she said. "He was bad today and threw his tea on me, didn't he?" She spoke to him like a child.

He shook his head from side to side violently. Mari lay her hand on his forehead, saying "Hiro-chan, Hiro-chan, be my good boy, Hiro-chan," until he grew quiet.

"Now tell me, what do you want to eat for lunch?" she asked him. He cried out some syllables I couldn't understand, and Mari said, "No, Mrs. Kakiuchi is not here today. I will make you lunch today."

Hiroyuki beat his hands against the bed, and I saw that his hands were slender and beautiful, perfectly normal hands.

He howled and Mari told him, "Daddy isn't here either, so I'll make you a big soup, okay?"

I followed Mari back downstairs, all of my ideas about her gone in a dream. I watched her pour a packet of instant corn soup into boiling water, and add vegetables and a boiled egg. She carried the soup on a tray, and with the air of a person lost in faraway thought, she fed him, ducking out of the way when his arms flew out at her. She waited when he turned his face away, holding the bowl of soup in one hand, the spoon in the other. She looked out the window at the waving trees.

At the Mother Superior's funeral, Mari whispered to me that she wanted to go again to the nightclub with the cat bridges and monkey cemetery. The days were getting hot and I sweated, still in my long-sleeved uniform jumper. I wanted to go too, the place was a waking dream I almost hadn't believed. A tomb was being constructed behind the convent for the Mother Superior, and I imagined it being inhabited by the wispy monkeys from the nightclub.

We went on a Saturday night, we drank too much champagne and looked into the eyes of giant electric eels who seemed to be watching us. Our hostess wore a leopard suit and took us to a room which was an elaborate miniature theatre, where she changed into a sorceress and sang an anthem. The curtain fell and when it rose again she knelt in a bright kimono outside of a holographic temple, and she began to recite old poems from the ninth and tenth centuries. Another women in the wings of the stage played a shakuhachi, which she would throw aside and replace with a shamisen when things got heated. Our hostess lamented with her hands in the air a song of watching the lights of her beloved's promises flicker and go one by one out. Mari wiped tears from her eyes and pulled at my arm.

I caught sight of the bill this time, and realized that just to enter this place, the price was 50,000 yen. Mari gave the hostess her credit card. Instead of getting in a taxi, we started walking towards the outskirts of town. It was just beginning to get light, and we sat for awhile on the metal steps to the rear entrance of an old cinema. There was one bright star left and the sun was rising before the star disappeared.

We kept walking. Mari was wearing shoes with little heels which were hurting her so she took them off and carried them in her hand. We entered lush countryside, crossing a bridge over a muddy river, where a man in a reed hat

was climbing down the bank with a bamboo
pole in his hands. I could hear crickets, and
everywhere I looked was deep green. The roads
grew narrower and narrower, and the pines
began to be more frequent and thick.

At the side of the road was a wooden cart
loaded with ripe cucumbers. Mari stopped and
took two of them and handed me one. We
walked along chewing on them as the rosy sun
came out. There were little houses here and
there, and ladies out hanging laundry. The
high pitched warning bell of the suburban commuter densha began to ring, and the red train
sped by on the other side of the river.

We were still drunk, and full of adrenalin
from being up all night. We kept walking as the
morning advanced, until we were in the forest
of pines which separated the farm lands from
the Pacific ocean. We came upon a grassy clearing with some tall fruit trees and Mari stopped
to lean against one of them. I climbed one
partway and sat on the branch.

"Oh, look," Mari said, crouching in the grass. "Here
is a cute little green frog." I looked at it sitting in
her hand.

"Hey, there are more!" she cried. "They're
all over the place!"

I made as if to jump down and she said,

"Wait! Climb down carefully, and watch where you step."

All through the grasses were hundreds of delicate, bright green frogs with gold bellies. They felt cool against the skin of my forearms as I let them climb on me. Very carefully, we left the clearing and continued along the beach access road. We could hear the waves, and the cries of the seagulls. When we reached the beach I took off my shoes and left them, and we ran to the water's edge. The air was clean and full of salt and rainbows. Mari opened her arms as if to embrace the sea and then we ran along the shore until we fell down exhausted and out of breath.

We lay on the sand looking at the sky, still the deep blue of early morning. I felt the light hand of Mari Shimada against my side, and in my mind I saw myself in the high Pamirs looking up at the snow. I sensed the fragrance of fresh minty herbs growing wild all around me, and in this mountain garden I dreamed myself sleeping.

When I felt myself being shaken I opened my blinded eyes to the dark outline of Mari crouching above me.

"Get up! Get up! We're broiling!" she said urgently. My limbs were taut and stiff, my skin stretched itself too tightly over my body. I stood with difficulty, my head reeling, and looked up and down the glaring white sand. There were people here and there, some men flying kites and some others standing around a boat with a net. Mari's face was bright pink, and I watched her run to the water and bring up handfuls of it to splash on her face. I followed and did the same.

It was not until the next day that the pain came, my face and neck burning and scorching me. I felt nauseated and ravaged, lying in my tiny four-tatami yojohan over Mama's bar, the electric fan buzzing beside me like a giant mosquito. I closed my eyes and saw wooly tarantulas while great beads of sweat rolled out of me and down my sides. I tried to immerse my face in icy water but no sooner did I lift my head from the sink than the burning pain came back in full force.

I looked in the mirror and saw that my face had begun to blister. Finally I crept downstairs and outside. I went to Akojimaya pharmacy and showed myself to the woman in the white coat behind the counter.

She clapped her hand over her mouth and shook her head. "What ever got into you to let yourself be burned that way?" she reproached me.

"I fell asleep on the beach," I told her.

She gave me a bottle of calamine lotion and something in a long tube which smelled of metal.

"Consider yourself lucky that you are so young," she said as she rang up the register. "A few years older and you would have ruined your skin for life."

Dr. Shimada had given Mari something for her face and arms. She had told him she fell asleep in the roof garden and slept too long. We went to sit in the little tatami room, and Mrs. Kakiuchi brought Calpico soda and sliced nashi fruit in a bowl of ice water. She looked at my face and then at Mari's, but she didn't say anything.

"I have some pain killers, if you want one," said Mari. She gave me a tiny blue tablet and I swallowed it. Before too long I began to float, and we sat side by side in silence. Our burned skin had its own shared language. Hiroyuki pressed his shackled spirit against me and I shook him off like a hot blanket. When late evening came we got up and went out into the tiny garden, where we sat in canvas chairs as the sun went down, like two convalescents in a stylish sanitarium rushing with its near empty quiet.

A DISENCHANTED WISH

One humid, late afternoon in summer, I went for a walk along the edge of Lake Hamana. I carried a little punctured box in which to catch a cicada. The blue air rang with their singing, which was the sound of heat itself. I looked from the tall reeds swaying gently around the lake to the hillside of dry pines where the big insects would surely be hiding.

I was too old at 16 to be out hunting cicadas, but never having done it, I wanted to. It was something all children did, and as for the ones who lived in the city without trees, they could always *buy* a cicada on the top floor of Seibu department store, along with a tiny bamboo cage.

As I followed the curve of the lake I saw a very strange thing. I saw a frail, colorless man in a white dressing gown standing in the water up to his calves, out in the reeds. He stood completely still. Then slowly, he raised his frighteningly thin arms, and almost as if doing a breast stroke he parted the reeds on either side of himself. He lifted one foot up out of the lake, and like a heron, took a long step forward. I suppressed the desire to laugh and watched him make his stiff, slow journey through the reeds.

There was a sound behind me on the path and I turned around. Another man, also wearing only a white dressing gown, tip-toed along barefooted, every few steps stopping to lift one foot and examine the bottom. Then I noticed others, up in the pine trees weaving in and out of sight like ghosts, and bright shouts came from the walled-in building above. Two nurses came clambering down the hill, waving their arms and shouting at the spirits in the trees. I looked around and saw that except for me and the ones in the gowns, there were no people about, here at this place hidden from the lake by the tall sighing reeds. One of the nurses bounded towards the one looking at his feet, glancing at me quickly as she took hold of him. He started to giggle, pressing his hands to the sides of his head.

"Have we got everybody?" the one on the hill shouted down, circling her little group like a sheep dog.

"No!" cried the one near me. "Mr. Yokoi is still missing!"

Holding the little box in my hands, I stole a glance at the lake, where the heron-man stood stock still, with one foot raised up out of the water.

I crept close to one of the trees, where on a wide branch sat an enormous green-brown cicada. It was impossible to isolate the place from where the clear, almost deafening sound came, shrill and crystalline, like glass. I held my breath, expecting the bug to notice me, spread his crisp, wide wings and fly away. But he sat obliviously on the branch, and I closed my box around him. All at once his singing stopped. A film of dampness covered my face, and I climbed back down to the path. The late red sun was behind me, and I put the box to my ear. A woman came out of the public restroom and walked toward me, wearing a short summer evening dress and black pumps. She had very white skin, and wore red lipstick and sunglasses. Over her shoulder she carried a large black bag. I had the feeling of knowing her somehow, and indeed, when she saw me a smile flew to her face.

"You don't remember me?" she asked, still smiling, and all at once I did.

"From the bar?"

She nodded. "Momoe," she introduced herself, and she bowed her head a little. Her hair was cut in a perfect bob, and she was very pretty, if overly done. She wore very heavy makeup for summer, and I had never before seen her in the daylight. I remembered her from a bar I had gone to from time to time, and she had always been very friendly. She was the one who liked to quote from Barbarella in English. It was disorienting to find myself standing with her far from the city, in the long late afternoon shadows at Lake Hamana.

"I'm Hiromi," I said.

"How do you do," Momoe said in mock formality, her voice husky.

"I live nearby," she said, gesturing vaguely in the direction of an unfamiliar neighborhood, little shimmering houses in the distance with blue-tiled roofs.

I felt embarrassed by my reason for being there, my little box with the sad cicada inside.

"I live in town," I said, "but I sometimes come out here on the bus."

Momoe nodded her head and said, "Well, I'm going to the bar, so why don't we ride the bus together." She shifted her bag to her other shoulder, and following my gaze up towards the building concealed in the blackening trees said,

"That's the loony bin up there. The patients are always escaping and coming down to the lake."

"Mr. Yokoi!" the voice of the nurse cried. "I can see you now very clearly in those reeds!"

We walked along the dusty road together, past little wooden buildings with awnings rolled out. A confectionery, a greengrocer, a bait and tackle shop. At the bus stand Momoe dropped coins into a vending machine and bought two iced coffees. I thanked her, realizing how very thirsty I was, as the blue and white stripe of the shinkansen flashed by in the distance on its way to Tokyo. There in the bleeding colors of the evening, in the remote rice field neighborhood near the lake, I had the peculiar, heady sensation of floating. I looked at Momoe's rather large, beautifully manicured hands. She was almost too glamorous, standing there at the curve of the road in her evening dress with the iced coffee, and for a moment I was reminded of an actress from the Takarazuka. When I saw the lights of the bus approaching I opened the little box and released the quiet cicada.

The bus was nearly empty and we sat together in the rear. Momoe told me that she was a student of mathematics at the university, and I can't say exactly why this surprised me, but it did. I mentioned that I was on summer holiday from high school, but not from which one. I was glad that she didn't ask me what I was or where I came from. That way I didn't have to explain right from the start about my dead Japanese Grandpa and his severed head. Instead, Momoe talked all about the books she liked, throwing in an American title here and there like Catcher in the Rye, among all the Tanizaki and Dazai and Soseki's I Am a Cat.

"Have you read Tanizaki's books?" Momoe asked me as we bounced along on the plush, magenta colored bus seats.

"Well," I answered painfully, "I can't read well enough to really enjoy books. I have to use a kanji dictionary."

Momoe frowned, then she laughed affably and lay her hand casually on my knee.

"I could always read them to you," she said. "Would you like that?"

A curious sliver of moon had materialized in the sky and followed the bus. We passed a gaudy pink love hotel with tall, pointed turrets. I looked at her face as shadows flashed over it from outside, and a current of something between fear and excitement went through me.

"Yes," I said, "I'd like that very much."

The nighttime streets bustled in the electric pleasure district. A small crowd had gathered outside the Paris Boulangerie to watch two girls with white-bleached hair and glitter eye makeup gesture at the cars inching past. One of them kept crouching down with a plastic bag and inhaling out of it, and I saw the ethereal whites of her eyes when she got to her feet.

In front of her bar, Momoe said almost nervously, "Maybe I'll see you again very soon, to read to you I mean." I nodded, feeling inhabited by a little army of anxious harpies. We stood awkwardly for another moment and then I said, "Well anyway, it was nice to see you again." Momoe smiled.

"Maybe I'll see you tomorrow night, on the roof of Sago department store."

She turned to go into the bar. "Maybe you will," I said, and music floated out when she opened the door.

I began to walk along the crowded street, past the bars, record shops, and pachinko parlours, at once thrilled and full of apprehension. Something about Momoe had left me unsettled, something I couldn't quite identify. I felt the ghost of her hand on my thigh and had to stop and lean against a parked car. In my hand I still clutched the little box I had taken to the lake.

It was deep summer, I was living in a yojohan above a little bar. I was like a light feather
on a gust of wind. The nuns from the school
were not aware of the exact nature of my cir-
cumstances, although Kaisei High School had
official custody of my visa. The head mistress
came downtown from Shijimizuka exactly once
each year, to buy a pair of new shoes at Marui,
the cheapest department store. She was not
familiar with any of the local restaurants and
probably imagined that my guardian owned one
that looked like Beni, the beautiful four star
place where tourists went. All she knew was
that my guardian was a "friend" of my mother
who was at home in the states, unmarried,
working many hours at her drawing table to pay
my expensive tuition. The Mother Superior,
then in her eighties, was satisfied with my
mother's letter of permission to let me stay in
town. Had the nuns known that this so-called
restaurant was actually a run-down little bar
serving Yakisoba and lots of whiskey to factory
workers and prostitutes, they would have
turned to powder. The Mama-san of the place
did try to look after me at first, but it wasn't
long before she gave up. As long as I paid her
the small amount of rent she required for the
yojohan and stayed out of trouble in her vicin-
ity, she kept her eyes averted.

To say that one's parents were divorced was

a supreme embarrassment. So I was in the habit of saying that my father had died. I could hardly tell the truth: that I'd never met my father because in fact he and my mother had met only once. Even the school officials were unaware of that. My mother made good money as a fashion illustrator for Nordstrom, and as far as the registrar was concerned, her being half-Japanese and called Misuzu excused her from certain questions. It didn't matter that she spoke hardly any Japanese and had spent her entire life in Seattle. Unlike me, my mother at least looked Japanese.

I realized that Momoe had not mentioned a time. So I waited until it had gotten dark before going to Sago department store. The rooftop, which was an amusement park by day, at night became a festive beer garden with swinging colored lights. From there you could look down on the vibrant city with its hypnotic neon signs and their metamorphosis into picture after picture; at once a flashing camera, rippling into a striped arrow, then the flashing camera again. And sitting on its wall of great stone blocks was the old castle, dwarfed by twinkling office buildings, and the zoo, all glimmering and scintillating from the breezy rooftop. I sat down at a little table and ordered an iced coffee.

I sat there for almost an hour, flipping anxiously through a magazine. Just as I was feeling impatient enough to leave, I felt a hand on my sleeve. I looked up at the face of a strange man. He sat down across from me. "It's me," he said. "Momoe." The voice was almost the same, and while I felt disbelief, it wasn't altogether shocking. The funny feeling I'd had was explained in an instant.

"Are you surprised?" he asked. I looked at his hands, the same smooth, graceful hands, but without the painted nails. He smiled, and that too, was the same. I felt as if I were meeting Momoe's brother. He didn't wait for me to answer.

"I didn't intend to startle you," he said, "but tonight I didn't have a chance to change. And I knew that I would have to tell you eventually anyway. This is always the tricky part, telling people the whole story."

He waved down the waitress.

"I'll have a beer," he told her, and he used the most masculine form of "I".

He also ordered a whiskey for me, although I didn't particularly feel like having one. I stared at him across the table, feeling suddenly very chilly. As a man he was small and almost scrappy, while Momoe was elegant and glamorous. He brought out a pack of Mild Sevens and offered me one. There was no trace of her in his gestures or manner, yet when I accepted a cigarette and he smiled, I was reminded of her. A lonely mist came down around me, making it difficult to clearly see him sitting there. There was a hush in my head, and inwardly I could hear myself calling out soundlessly, the way voices are muted in deeply fallen snow.

"I live with my mother, you see," he told me when the drinks came. "Oh, and my real name is Tetsuya." He lit a cigarette.

"I live out near Lake Hamana, but my mother doesn't know that I'm a cross-dresser. So I have to go to that public restroom and change in there before I go to the bar. You see?"

I downed the whiskey in one swallow. I shook my head to clear the shadows. "How often do you go out dressed up like that?" I heard myself ask.

"Not very often," he answered. "Only when I work at the bar, and sometimes when I go out at night. I only work at the bar three nights. I'm a math student, remember."

"Are you a..." I hesitated, unsure of exactly what to ask.

Tetsuya laughed. "Am I an okama, you were going to ask me? That's a fair question, of

81

course! But no, I'm not an okama, I like women. I like them so much I enjoy actually becoming one. I like to feel the machine of the female psyche grinding away inside of me."

He ordered more drinks. "And I like the way that normal men treat me differently, thinking that I'm a woman. To the average man, whatever looks like a pretty woman is just that. So you see, I take a real anthropological interest in my cross-dressing."

Tetsuya lit another cigarette. I found myself not liking him, which confused me since I had liked Momoe. Momoe had a graceful reserve, a shy gentleness that I liked. And she had an extreme, if not exaggerated, femininity. I felt a hot anger sweep up around me and tried to cool it with the icy whiskey.

Suddenly the beer garden seemed ridiculous, crowded with tables of drunk salarymen served by sullen waitresses in silly Bavarian-style smocks. I was feeling the whiskies, but not pleasantly. Instead my limbs felt cumbersome and I wanted to climb out of the burden of my body and fly lightly up into the glowing night sky. Tetsuya called the waitress and ordered another beer, offering me another whiskey. I shook my head and stood up.

"I have to go now," I said. He looked up, flushed and surprised.

"Why?"

"I have to get up early tomorrow," I lied. It was a pale lie nobody would have believed, and I didn't care.

"Well," said Tetsuya, almost with annoyance, "I'll give you money for a taxi."

He reached into his pocket for his wallet.

"No thank you," I said, "I don't live far from here."

I said goodbye and started to walk toward the little elevator house. Tetsuya got up abruptly and grabbed hold of my hand. I looked at him, his bright, rather intoxicated eyes glittering, and he said,

"I know you like Momoe better than me. You like girls better than boys anyway."

Then he let go of my hand and went back to the table. I rode the fluorescent elevator to the street with a spike of alarm in my heart. He was right, in fact; I did prefer Momoe to him. But that seemed absurd, both of them being the same person, after all. I stood on the street in front of the main entrance to Sago Department store, closed for the night except for its gaudy beer garden, watching the nighttime people walking languidly by. Some boys with greased hair passed me, wearing shimmering, outlandishly colored happi coats, and wooden geta loosely on their feet. They clattered past with cigarettes between their fingers, wearing wraparound sunglasses even though it was night.

In the morning I awoke early. There was noise coming from the bar downstairs, and I quickly folded my futon and pushed it into the cabinet. As I went to have a bath I could hear the radio playing softly in Mama-san's rooms where her husband was still asleep. I could hear his snoring as I poured water over myself. Then I dressed in shorts and a light cotton shirt and went downstairs. Obachan, Mama's mother, was in the bar cleaning. She had the vacuum going and the metal gate outside was pushed halfway up. She waved at me and smiled, pointed to a bowl of rice with a piece of fish on it sitting on the bar. I sat down to eat while Obachan finished vacuuming.

I remembered her peeking out shyly from the curtain separating the bar from the kitchen when I first came to live there. The way that she clapped her hand over her mouth when she smiled like a little girl. Once I had been there a short time, all of her shyness evaporated and in her deep whiskey and cigarette voice Obachan began telling me her stories. She reminded me of Simone Signoret somehow, and I told her that. Obachan laughed and said it was the nicest thing she'd heard in years.

She turned off the vacuum and wrapped up the cord. Then she poured herself a cup of coffee and sat beside me at the bar. "Eat that fish," she said, nudging me. "I fried it this morning, it's fresh." I pushed a piece of it into my mouth, the salt making my eyes water. She fanned herself with a Non-no magazine. "I wanted to get everything done before it gets too hot," she said, "before that lazy bum of a son-in-law wakes up and gets in my way." Mama-san's husband was an enigmatic sort of man who wore a green zip-up work uniform and worked somewhere late at night. He had the permed hair of a small-time yakuza, and wore a gold chain around his neck. I almost never saw him. Mama-san was like a younger version of her mother, content to work in the bar, to go out drinking once a week, once a month to the Kobe race track. And she only bet on Serpent Prince, whose picture was framed behind the bar.

I finished eating and Obachan took the bowl behind the bar. "I'll tell you one," she said, leaning on her elbows in front of me. "I drove a car once, imagine that?" I shook my head. "Well, you know I'm not very mechanical, but still, it was a new thing where I lived, way out in the weeds. It was about 1940, and there was this certain man." She raised her eyebrows and I smiled.

"He was somewhat of dandy, and he had a brand-new car. I don't remember the make, but it was a beauty. And he told me that if I would spend an afternoon with him, he would teach me how to drive it. So we went to Inuyama, and he let me drive on those mountain roads, winding higher and higher. Suddenly I panicked, it felt that we were going so fast, and he said, put the brake on, put the brake on, and I accelerated instead and drove through an oden cart. I can still see the poor oden seller leaping out of the way, and this poor man, not only did I crash his new car into the trees at the roadside, but he also had to pay the oden seller. And that was the last time I ever tried to drive."

"What happened to the man?" I asked her. She shook her head. "That's the haunting part. You see, I didn't ever see him again, but during the war, he became a Kamikaze pilot, and I remember his memorial. It was a local family. I kept thinking, when I heard that he had flown his plane into a warship, about me crashing his car into the oden cart. You should have seen his face when I couldn't stop that car! White like a mountain radish. I could not possibly imagine him having the courage to become a Kamikaze pilot." Obachan shook her head and lit a cigarette.

I was returning from a walk, and when I neared the door to Mama's bar I saw Momoe just coming out. She looked beautiful, and I felt wings beating in my chest when she caught sight of me. She was wearing a short black skirt with a crisp linen jacket and tall black pumps. She smiled at me apologetically, and I fought the impulse to take hold of her hand. The relief of looking at her there before me made me almost want to cry.

"Can I please buy you an iced coffee?" Momoe offered. She pursed her lips, and the restraint I had bottled inside of me fell from its safe place in my reason and spilled. I followed Momoe to a little upstairs place in Sakanamachi with only three or four tables. The owner was someone she knew, a little effeminate man called Shuichi, with unpleasantly thick lips. He served us iced coffees and chatted for a moment about all the money he had just lost at the track.

Momoe smiled at me. Then she opened her pocketbook and took out her cigarettes and lighter. I studied her face, powdered and smooth, black eyeliner and mascara, and deep red lips. She exhaled and said, "I really am sorry about last night. I should have told you myself rather than just showing up like that. Or perhaps I shouldn't have told you at all."

"What did you mean when you said that I like girls better anyway?" I asked her.

"I meant. . ." She hesitated, grinding out her cigarette. "Well, from what I saw at the bar, it seemed that you like girls, you know."

"No," I said, my chest hollowing itself out around the alarm which was becoming more and more familiar. "I don't know. What exactly did you see there?"

I watched Momoe's face, her eyes widening and narrowing as she recounted an evening lost to me in the fogbanks of drunkenness. Everything around her was swallowed up in blackness, leaving only her white-powdered face in my eyes, a strange and unthinkable noh drama unfolding from her about me, an unspeakable, outlandish tale in dark pictures. A vanished memory floated past as faint as an echo, of peculiar sounds and intimate gestures, aberrant fragments of shameful declarations. "I thought you'd bite her tongue off," Momoe was saying. *I thought you'd bite her tongue off.* I tried fruitlessly to isolate my place in the drama, faced only with a grainy picture of myself in a nebulous embrace. Momoe had finished speaking, and I sat with my hand pressed to my mouth. I felt feverish.

"Oh, now don't go getting all upset about it," Momoe said, laughing softly. "It was all in fun, and nobody minded. You seemed to be liking it, as much as that other girl, and nobody got hurt. I just thought that you might like me a little, Momoe, I mean. I won't see you again as a man. It's so much nicer this way, don't you think?" My hands trembled as I lit one of Momoe's cigarettes and looked out the window.

The first gift Momoe gave me was her gold cigarette lighter. It was plain and elegant. All I said was that I liked it and Momoe had emphatically cried, "Then I want you to have it!" and pressed it into my hand. "Remember me with it," she added. The second gift was a translated copy of The Makioka Sisters by Junichiro Tanizaki. It came through the mail with no card or letter. She had not yet read aloud to me from her own Japanese edition, but I found myself wanting her to. There were lots of gifts after that, all in a very short time.

One day I went with Momoe to a pachinko parlor on the outskirts of town. She sat at a machine between two men in suits, flicking the lever furiously, and unloading a landslide of little silver balls into her plastic tub. She stood up and motioned for me to follow her to the cashier. She had won enough to trade in for a watermelon. She spoke in such a clear, feminine way, and her manners, the way she walked, they were like the most prominent actresses in the movies. I wanted so much for her to be

only her. And strangely, it was her very femininity that would suddenly and unwelcomely
remind me that she was actually a man. After
playing pachinko that day, Momoe took me for
a drive in her mother's Cedric. She took me to
the auto races at Fuji Speedway near the
mountain, to see the Austin Mini Cooper race.
We watched little cars tearing around the race-
track, and I laughed out loud. Momoe laughed
too, with her hand on my shoulder. On the way
back, we stopped at a roadside restaurant for a
hamburger. Momoe went into the ladies' room
to fix her make-up. Her going in there seemed
almost too brazen, too exaggerated. After all,
she was still a man under all that Kanebo face
powder, and a man who might like to listen to
women pee, for all I knew. When she came
back to the table, in the big crowded restaurant
full of travelers, she said,

"I would like to give you a big kiss, but all
these people would look at us." Then she
laughed and bit into her hamburger. I imagined
her kissing me and felt as if I might lose consciousness.

On the way back we drove through lush
green rice fields with old thatch-roofed farm
houses. We could see farm ladies in their wide
blue pantaloons bent over working in the damp
green. Momoe beeped the horn at an old lady
near the edge of her field beside the road,

and the sun glistened on her gold smile as we passed. I can still see Momoe raising her hand to wave, and her lovely smile, her elusive dimple.

"They're sweet, these bumpkins," she said, looking at me and biting her lip. The look fluttered my heart for an instant and then it calmed again. Momoe lay her hand on my knee as she drove onto the highway, passing a stern-faced artificial policeman standing on the grassy shoulder.

With the pines blackening and the sun purple we drove to the beach with Yumi Arai singing on the radio, and the silver ocean spread out before us. Momoe drove onto the beach and turned off the engine. She turned to me, the leather seat creaking in the hard silence of the car.

"Come on, just let me give you one little tiny kiss," she said, and she leaned over and touched her lips almost imperceptibly to mine. I stopped breathing.

"Don't be afraid of me," she said, pulling away. "Oh look, you have some of my lipstick." She rubbed my lips with her thumb.

"I can't imagine anyone being afraid of me," said Momoe.

The half-moon floated out over the sea.

"When I was a child," she said, "I was always the smallest boy. And the bigger ones tormented me on the way home from school. They would push me into Lake Hamana. Once, I remember, they tied my hands behind me, and bound my feet together and then they carried me out into the tall reeds up to my chest in water and left me there. I was so afraid that I would slip under and drown, and it took me what felt like forever to get to the shore. It was getting dark, and some patients from the mental institution had come down to the edge of the lake in their pajamas and I thought they were swamp ghosts."

Momoe laughed at the memory. "I was so terrified, half frozen and soaked. One of them came walking toward me, reaching out to me, and I tried to scream but only air came out of me. All he did was untie my hands! I wanted to run but I still had my feet to untie, and the boys had used a cloth headband to bind them, which was soaked and impossible to undo. So I sat on the ground in my wet clothes with the swamp ghost saying 'Poor little turtle,' over and over to me, until another one came with the lid of an eel-tin he had found, and used it to cut through the cloth. Then I ran home, crying. I didn't even thank them. I realized much later that the gentle swamp ghost must have seen the boys taunting me other times along the lake, perhaps from his window in the mental institution. He must have called me 'little turtle' like the one in the story of Urashima Taro. Do you know that story?"

Momoe looked at me, raising her eyebrows. I knew the story, but I shook my head anyway. It was growing dark, and the sea looked like mica.

"Once there was a kindhearted boy called Urashima Taro." I listened to the waves and to Momoe's voice. "He was a good boy from a little fishing town, probably like this town was once, before Pizza Hut and video parlours came. One day when he was walking on the beach, he came upon some mean boys tormenting a big turtle with sticks. He chased them away and waited until the turtle had swum far out into the water before going home. Some days later, he was on the beach daydreaming when he heard a voice calling him, and he saw it was the turtle. The turtle thanked Urashima Taro for rescuing him, and as a present in return, he offered to take him on a ride under the sea on his back."

Momoe paused to offer me a cigarette, and we each lit one.

"So, Urashima Taro, he was a very adventurous person like you. And he climbed onto the turtle's back and rode to the bottom of the sea. He was amazed at what a beautiful place it was, and the turtle took him to a magnificent undersea garden where there was a splendid castle. There Urashima Taro met a gorgeous ohimesama, and he fell in love with her. He stayed for three years, and he was very happy. But, little by little, he started to feel homesick for his family and friends in his town, and he told the ohimesama he wanted to go back to visit them. She called the turtle to take him back, and before he left, she gave him a small box and told him, whatever happens, you must never ever open this box. Then Urashima Taro climbed onto the turtle and rode up out of the magic undersea kingdom to the land. On the beach, he said goodbye to the turtle, and carrying the little box he went into the village. He found everything completely changed and felt very bewildered. Approaching a man in the street, he asked him,

"Excuse me. Do you know the house of Urashima Taro?"

The man was quite surprised by the question and said,

"But Urashima Taro has been dead for 300 years. He is a legend here."

Urashima Taro was shocked when he heard this, and he realized that for every year he passed under the sea, a century had passed on the land. Very sad, he went back to the beach and sat down on the sand with the box the ohimesama had given him. All at once he decided to ignore what she said and open the box. When he did an enormous plume of smoke, like a cloud, came out of the box and enveloped him. When the smoke cleared around Urashima Taro, he was an old, old man with a long, long white beard."

Momoe sighed. "Well, what do you think of that?" she said. I saw lustrous pictures all around her from her stories, and my trepidation had melted away.

"I think," I said, "that you are like the turtle, Urashima Taro *and* the lovely ohimesama."

Momoe smiled modestly, and for a moment I thought she might embrace me. But she reached instead into the back seat for her makeup bag and took out a little pair of scissors.

"I want to eat that watermelon," she said, "and this is all I have to cut it with." She got out of the car and took the melon from the back. She spread a page of The Mainichi Shimbun over the seat and cut into the rind.

"Too bad we don't have the lid of an eeltin," I said and she smiled.

"You know," she said, "when I was a kid I always took off every stitch of clothing in the back garden to eat watermelon, but I won't do that this time."

I climbed out of the car and she handed me a jagged piece of melon, dripping juice onto the pale sand.

The next several days I didn't see or speak to Momoe. It was hot and wet, and I passed the most intense parts of my afternoons in air-conditioned movie houses and coffee bars. One afternoon, the planes from the Air Force flew in elaborate precision over the town. In the tiny backyard behind Mama's bar, Obachan cramped her neck looking up at them in the pale sky. Mama-san gave me some money to buy some Tokuhon Chill at the pharmacy. When I returned with the little parcel, my spirits flew like the planes when I saw Momoe seated at the bar, watching Mama stirring up yakisoba. I could have laughed out loud watching Mama serve her politely and obliviously, noting that Mama was not nearly as attractive as Momoe, and probably hadn't been even when she was Momoe's age. Momoe turned and winked at me, breaking apart her wooden chopsticks. I said hello to her then went through the curtain to the kitchen where Obachan sat rubbing her neck. "Ahh!" she exclaimed, taking the parcel and opening it. The room filled

with camphor as Obachan rubbed the Tokuhon
Chill on her sore neck. Then I went back out
into the bar. Mama was chatting casually with
Momoe about the heat, leaning on the bar
drinking a Coca Cola. I sat down at one of the
empty tables and looked out at the bright
street. Mama turned on the radio and looked at
the newspaper. After Momoe had finished eating, she opened her pocketbook and took out a
small mirror and her lipstick, which she applied
discreetly, turning away from the bar. Mama
took a broom and went out onto the sidewalk,
leaving the two of us momentarily alone in the
bar.

"Oi," Momoe said, snapping her pocketbook closed. "You want to go out tonight, to a
different kind of place?"

"What sort of place?" I asked. She narrowed her eyes mysteriously.

"It's a little underground place. It's called
Harajuku. It's one of those kind of places, you
know." She leaned forward and whispered, "An
okama place. I'll take you if you like."

The idea of a forbidden, underground place
full of okamas was enthralling.

"Of course I want to go there," I told her,
and my head swam with conjured images.
Momoe told me to meet her at 10:00 at

Shuichi's bar, and then she went out and disappeared.

Mama-san offered me a yakisoba but it was too hot to eat much of anything. I sliced a nashi fruit and then I went to my room and fell asleep beside the electric fan.

I wasn't at all sure of what to wear, so I just put on a short black dress with no sleeves. I had no shoes like the kind Momoe wore, and had to make do with sandals. I wished that I had something a little more elegant, but I didn't. Before going out, I put on some eyeliner and lipstick, and tucked some money into my little bag. Then I walked to Sakanamachi and waited on the sidewalk in front of Shuichi's bar. When Momoe came, she said, "It's still too early, so let's wait upstairs awhile."

We went and sat at a table and Shuichi greeted us. "You look very pretty tonight," he said, and turning to Momoe said, "Doesn't she?" Momoe glittered and ordered two whiskies. We drank those and ordered more. Shuichi brought us doubles.

"What are you doing tonight?" he asked, setting the glasses on the table. I was hypnotized by the flashy Hawaiian shirt he wore.

"I'm taking Hiromi to Harajuku later," Momoe answered, lighting a Mild Seven.

Shuichi's eyes widened, and his thick lips stretched into a big smile. He shook his finger at me and said, "You should watch out in that dive, you're going to be the main attraction." He leapt at Momoe, like a little jumping spider, and slapped her hand. "You'd better protect her. You'd better pretend you're *avec*, if you know what I mean." He threw his head back and laughed, and then went behind the bar with his tray. The alcohol was rushing through my bloodstream and I felt my face burn. Shuichi brought more whiskey, and I felt myself beginning to lose my grip.

When it was time, Momoe led me down narrow winding streets I had never taken, through passageways hung with laundry, past back entrances to tiny restaurants issuing clouds of steam, women in gaudy dresses applying makeup in doorways. We seemed to be walking in circles. I stumbled along behind Momoe in the poorly lit street with all its shops closed and shuttered. Finally she turned into a doorway. A long, tight corridor led to a staircase at the end, and at the bottom another corridor led us to a black door. Momoe knocked, and a little window slid open. The eyes behind it swept over us like a search light, then the door opened. A stout woman in heavy makeup stood aside, and Momoe greeted her formally, taking a 5000 yen note from her pocket book. "Thank you, baby," said the woman in a deep male voice. She pulled back a heavy curtain and motioned us in saying, "Irashyai."

We entered a crowded, smoky little bar-room, with candles burning on the tables. Outlandishly dressed men stood at the bar, and on the tiny dance floor I saw boys with their arms wrapped around each other and their lips pressed together. Momoe took me by the hand and led me through the room, waving to two very obvious boys in dresses sitting at a table. One of them had a prominent Adam's apple and enormous hands spread out on the table. We sat down on a sofa before a porno movie playing on a soundless television screen. A slender boy with thick lashes came to take our drink order. Momoe ordered a bottle. She dropped ice cubes into the glasses and placed one hand on my thigh. She raised her glass of whiskey and said, "Kampai," while I took hold of mine almost desperately.

A tall, magical beauty materialized in the curtained doorway. I watched her dress glittering and flashing with all its sequins as she approached, and as she passed us she winked, and I noticed her long, long lashes. I watched her disappear again through another curtain, the wink still fluttering in the air where she had been.

"Was that a man?" I asked Momoe.

"Yes," Momoe said, "she is, and she's very famous."

Three women with slick hair had come in and sat down around a table, their legs wide apart. They were ugly, like ugly men, even in the way they held their cigarettes. One of them suddenly caught my eyes with hers and sucked her teeth. I looked quickly back in the other direction, where the lovely sequined creature had disappeared, and to Momoe.

On the TV screen, a woman's face was twisted in an agony of ecstasy, and then she appeared to hyperventilate as if giving birth, and the camera pulled back to reveal another woman, sliding around her lower parts, kissing something that had been mechanically blurred out. Then they had their faces together, kissing with lots of tongue and hair tossing, their mouths opening widely as if they were screaming. I didn't take my eyes from the screen as I drained my glass of whiskey. Momoe sat quietly beside me, rubbing my thigh and pouring me more whiskey. The room pulsated, changing colors with the light from the TV screen. I closed my eyes and was pulled into a whirlpool of sumptuous visions; butterflies with lime velvet wings floating down onto glass-frozen water, a wild tree of icy monkeys.

The waiter with thick lashes leaned over me, talking to Momoe. "I can't stand the Candies," Momoe was saying, "Can't you put on another record?"

"OK," the boy said, disappearing. Momoe pulled me back into the other room and onto the dance floor, under spiraling lights like snowflakes falling all around us, and we danced to some other kind of music, something that was lost as soon as it came. The room was all sound and color and Momoe's pretty face close to mine. Once again I was reminded of the Takarazuka, and I let her kiss me, a kiss that made me close my eyes and see myself running alongside an endless stone wall overgrown with vegetation. I looked at her and deep down in the black well of my imagination, a vague fear glistened faintly. She was a predatory violet, she was disco music interrupted by the plucking of a biwa. My legs weakened, and I let myself be taken outside. Fresh air came at me like little wings in the sudden hush of the street.

"Let me take you to a love hotel." Momoe's voice pressed into me. She coaxed me with her hands around my neck, her smile and her lustrous eyes. She pulled a taxi out of my drunken oblivion, and I climbed in beside her. The nighttime city lights rushed past the windows in great stripes, and then quiet came, cool air and the singing of cicadas. The taxi let us off in front of a garish fairy tale castle. Momoe led me into the subdued lobby, and I waited in a chair next to the elevators.

The room we entered was an old chapel, with luminous stained glass windows and a bank of flickering candles. I went to them and realized that they were all electric. There was a dimmer switch beside them and I turned it, making the candles go from bright to dim several times. I climbed upon the tall, four poster bed and Momoe disappeared for what seemed like a long time and I fell into a light sleep. I felt her climb up onto the bed, and saw that she wore only her slip and sheer stockings. She was freshly made up, and somewhere deep within, a voice called out telling me to stop. Momoe kissed me, and started unbuttoning my dress. She smelled velvety, and like Kali seemed to have hands everywhere. She pulled away to look at me, smiling gently, with her dimple and glittery eyes. I floated along on a soft current, enveloped by her, feeling her hands between my thighs. I slept while being awake, my eyes closed as she lay on me, pulling off my underclothes. I opened my eyes and looked at her face, elucidated by the glowing colored windows and shimmering electric candles, and then without warning I felt only pain, a sudden suffering that made my heart stop. Momoe hoisted herself up on both arms, and clarity rushed into the room like cold air.

"Momoe," I murmured, wanting it to stop. But Momoe was nowhere, vanished like a disenchanted wish, and I looked at the smeared lipstick and beaded sweat on the mask-like face above me. I felt the sweat fall on my skin, thick and gluey with the rice-powder makeup. On her glistening chin I saw the bluish shadow of a close shave, and closed my eyes again. I tried to set free my thoughts, to push them up and out of my body away from the relentless pain forcing its way into me. I listened to an unknown rasping sound breathed into my ear and Momoe shuddered, then fell damply onto me. I throbbed, and streaks of sharp pains shot up to my heart, snaking around it and returning to the source. I felt myself expelling him in a sickening warm wetness. He lay motionless beside me and I pulled myself into a tight curl.

At some point I woke to find her sitting on the bed looking at me, her face repaired, and her clothes intact.

She said quietly, "It wasn't as if you were really with a man exactly, and the good thing is, it won't ever hurt again. The worst is over, baby." I looked at her but couldn't bring her fully into focus. I only saw Tetsuya, sitting there in face powder, lipstick and overdone mascara. I reached out and pulled the wig off, and there he was. A slight little man carefully shaved, on the face, under the arms.

Just before school started again, I went back to Lake Hamana. It looked the same as it had that first day, and the reeds whispered, swaying back and forth in the breeze along the water's edge. The cicadas were singing, but without their former brilliance, perhaps sensing the changing of the seasons about to come.

There were no swamp ghosts in sight, and I climbed the hill into the pine trees, their needles pricking my skin. I stood very still, listening. Then I turned my head and looked at a little cicada close by on a tree. I reached out and closed it into my hand.

THE PNEUMATIC LANTERNS

Eriko, the little one with the mischievous face, approached me one evening as I folded my hakama in the small zinc-roofed changing house.

"What is the English word for the female sexual organ?" she wanted to know.

"Do you mean the slang word?" I asked her.

Her funny wide smile rushed to her lips.

"No, I mean the clinical word."

"Okay," I said, "the word is vagina."

Eriko's hand flew over her mouth and she laughed. There is no letter V in the Japanese language.

"Say it one more time."

"Vagina."

She laughed again. "Bajaina," she said. "Is that right?"

"Why do you want to know this word," I asked her.

"Because," she said, "it isn't in my dictionary."

It was winter and terribly cold. The changing house for the youngest members of the kendo club was unheated, sitting out behind the dojo. I was 15 then, a first year student at Kaisei High School. The sempai, the older girls (our superiors), had their own heated changing rooms inside the dojo, where we would bring them tea, and their clean linens, which we washed by hand in big metal tubs in the laundry room and hung up to dry. That night I had a bloody blister on my foot from the chilled dojo floor. Eriko went with me to the infirmary, down a dark hallway with the sliding wooden doors of silent classrooms closed on either side, toward the glowing red exit lamp at the end.

The buildings of Kaisei Catholic High School were like a maze constructed in wood, with glass windowpanes melted with age, all connected by long drafty hallways and staircases.

The infirmary was painted a rosy color. It

was a room out of the last century, with the two white iron bedsteads and the big porcelain bowl on a stand near the tall windows. Glass jars full of metal instruments and cotton sat on a table, and on the wall above the two beds an enormous crucifix was hung, with blue gem-tears spilling from the eyes of Christ over his creamy cheeks. When we entered the room, Sister White looked up from where she sat reading at her little enamel table. She was named for the white habit she wore, embellished with a red cross on her breast. Toothy and clever, she was young and much less stern than the other nuns.

"Soon I won't be here to wrap your feet anymore," she said, smiling sadly.

"What's that?" asked Eriko.

"I am going to Tokyo to study," she said, "and you will all be very kind to my replacement, won't you."

"Yes, Sister," we said, even though she'll probably be an old onibaba, we were thinking.

Sister White left the school without celebration, and the replacement arrived unnoticed. When I met her I was surprised to see someone young and strong looking. She was not a nun, and was called Suzuki-Sensei. The very first time she touched me, I had a long thick sliver of wood embedded in my heel. It came out of the wooden slats laid over the ice between the dojo and our changing house. It went into me so violently and swiftly that I screamed out, feeling that my heart might stop because it hurt so much. As soon as I realized what had happened, the already dark sky went velvety and black and the cold air brushed my cheeks as I slipped to the frozen ground. Big Tomoko and Eriko rushed out of the changing house.

"Her face is completely white!" shouted Big Tomoko.

"Put out some energy!" shrieked Eriko as they helped me to stand up. The night spun all around me.

"Something has pricked my foot deeply," I told them, as they half carried me over the slick wooden floorboards of the hallway, toward the flickering red exit lamp. In the infirmary, Big Tomoko approached the new nurse. She bowed and said,

"Excuse us, Sensei, but this girl has gotten a spike of wood deeply planted into her foot." She turned to indicate me, standing in the doorway with Eriko. Eriko held onto my arm. She looked like a praying mantis, all big-eyed.

"Well, all right," Suzuki-Sensei said

brusquely. "Come in and sit down."

I went and sat on the edge of one of the white beds. Turning to Eriko and Big Tomoko, she said,

"You can go now. She can talk for herself, I'm quite sure."

They both bowed awkwardly and went out. I saw a flash of Eriko's face at the dark window in the door as it swung closed. My entire leg throbbed.

Suzuki-Sensei knelt down and held my foot in both her hands to examine my heel. She drew in a breath through her teeth and I had to close my eyes. Then she let go, and I listened to her opening the jars on the metal table and felt the sharp sting of alcohol in my nose. She pulled over a stool and perched on it with a pair of long thin tweezers in her hand.

"Now sit very quietly," she said, and she touched my foot with the tweezers. I flinched involuntarily. She stopped, my foot resting in her lap, and stared up at me.

"Haven't you any more strength than that?"

She looked right into my eyes so that I was forced to look away.

"I'm sorry, Sensei," I said, and felt my face

and neck get hot. She did not look Japanese, really. Her features were severe and unusual, like a Mongolian. I imagined her on a fierce tiny Mongolian horse and suddenly felt terribly self-conscious about my rough, blistered foot lying in her smooth brown hands. Then fire burst through my foot and up my leg.

"Atari!" she exclaimed, holding up the spike. "You see, Hiromi-san, it is a little nothing."

"It is a branch," I said, shocked to hear her say my name. I felt her eyes walking all over my face, and I saw a smile flutter momentarily at her lips as she massaged my foot.

I was sitting with my legs folded beneath me on the cold red tiles outside the library. The door to the library was in the center of the second floor hallway of the second year building. There was another girl sitting a few feet away, staring at the floor with her face all ashamed. I wondered what she was being punished for. I had been late again that morning and sentenced with a whack of Sister Kawaguchi's pen to one hour directly following after-school cleanup. Some of the older girls who passed me on their way to the shoe room laughed behind their hands and winked at me.

I watched the sky darken through the big four-paned windows from where I sat with no

more sensation in my legs. When I stood up, I
had to stumble along the wall, down the
gloomy hallway, as my legs began to tingle
painfully. I went down the stairs to the first
floor and followed the corridor to the outside
yard. I ran along the edge of the dirt tennis
court, flooded with light. Suzuki-Sensei was
coaching Sister White's tennis club in the
freezing cold. She had on blue sweatpants and
a sweatshirt with the sleeves rolled up to her
forearms. I was used to seeing Sister White,
her endless fabric like a swollen sail, slamming
the tennis ball with all her might, and to catch-
ing glimpses of her short, short hair under her
wimple.

"Kimpara-san! Watch your backhand!"
Suzuki-Sensei shouted, and I felt a violent jolt
like a rifle discharging in my chest as I hurried
toward the dojo. I could hear the loud cries
coming out of the glowing building, and the
blows of all the many feet against the floor.

Two nights a week I had a secret job. I was
a waitress in a tiny kissaten in the
Sakanamachi district. It was on the second
floor above a beauty salon, and had big tinted
windows along the stairs so that I was able to
keep an eye on who was coming up before they
could see clearly in. This was an advantage
since having any sort of job, especially in a

kissaten, was strictly off limits according to the rules of Kaisei High School. In fact, just sitting in kissaten or bar was an offense punishable by expulsion if you were caught. The only allowable coffee shops were the big antiseptic ones on the top floors of department stores. I was taking more of risk than I realized at the time. There were certain non-Catholic teachers who roamed those streets in shifts, looking for familiar faces. Had I been discovered by Gokiburi-Sensei (Mr. Cockroach), who had an uncanny ability to be everywhere at once, the consequences would have been immediate and remarkable.

At the kissaten in Sakanamachi I worked both with the owner, who was called Maki, and with another girl of about 19 named Chiemi, who had the face of a lemur. Maki was tall and elegant, and she wore her hair up in a French twist. She loved everything French, and had autographed photos of Alain Delon and Mireille Darc on the wall behind the little bar. She liked me because I looked different. She liked the fact that I had hardly any Japanese blood at all. I gave her little joint atmosphere, she said.

While Chiemi stood behind the bar pouring coffee and liquor and cutting up the cheesecakes she had made herself at home, I took orders from the six tiny tables. I was asked by almost every customer what I was and where I was from. Chiemi was full of demons and was very atmospheric herself. She was having an affair with a much older, married man, and she wore a mood ring. Her married man came in almost every night near closing time and sat at the bar to wait for her. He had a name, but he told me to call him Uncle.

"Hiromi can read palms," Chiemi told him one night. He turned his bull's face to me and held out his hand. He had on a dark gray suit. I looked at the many lines criss-crossing his palm and they blurred before my eyes.

"So? What can you see?" he asked me with a smile in his voice. Chiemi looked on with her chin in her hand.

"You have three kids," I guessed, while my mind was altogether elsewhere.

"That's right!"

"You have two daughters and one son."

"That's right again."

"Your son is shy and does terribly in math and can run fast."

Uncle raised his thick eyebrows.

"Amazing," he said, turning down the corners of his mouth. "This is all true what you just said."

I went to clear away the last table, my mind running back to an earlier part of the day. I had gone to have Suzuki-Sensei wrap my feet, sitting across from her on a chair. After wrapping them, she reached out and petted my hair with both hands, and I held my breath. She petted me while telling me how to take care of the blister on my foot, very matter-of-fact, as if she wasn't touching me at all. I cleared the cups and plates from the table, wondering if it had happened at all, or if I had only imagined her hands on my head.

Once again there were two pieces of Chiemi's cheesecake left with only one bite taken. This was the fifth time in one night it had happened.

"Look, Chiemi," I said when I brought the plates behind the bar. She frowned and cocked her head at the cake. "I'd better taste it," she said, and took a bite from one of the pieces. She made a face and cried, "I'm stupid! I forgot to put in sugar!"

After closing I went with Chiemi and Uncle to a bar called Prison. It was split into lots of little rooms with iron bars just like jail cells. Uncle kept his own bottle of whiskey there with his name on the label. The bottle wore its own little doll-size trench coat. The bar hostess brought the bottle into our cell with an ice bucket and three glasses. She was friendly, with a very deep voice and heavy makeup, and whenever I came in she would say in thickly accented English,

"You so pretty, Pretty-pretty," and then add in Japanese, "That's from a movie." She poured out three drinks. "Are you going to sing tonight?" she asked Uncle, smiling.

"I think I just might!" he said buoyantly. He stood up and went to the karaoke machine, loosening his tie.

"He likes to sing old-fashioned enka songs," said Chiemi, rolling her eyes. She poured me another whiskey and I downed it quickly. Uncle began to sing:

My Darling, why, why

Why did you just throw me away

Now here I sit

In this nighttime sake bar

All alone and crying

Chiemi showed me her mood ring turning from blue to black.

Because of the drinking it was hard to wake up in the morning. I ran to school with my head pounding. Roseate light bathed

Hamamatsu Castle, and crowded buses rumbled by. I got to school five minutes late and tore my shoes off in the shoe room. Shoving my indoor shoes under my arm, I ran in my stockings to the classroom. I had to slide the door open with an appalling screech as my classmates sang the opening hymn. Sister Kawaguchi did not look at me as I crept to my seat, but I could see her mental note being taken. All through her geography lesson I sat quietly ill. The big white canvas curtains blew into the room and settled again. My eyes felt like molten fish roe, and my stomach longed for cool air. I felt a sharp pinch on the underside of my arm and sat up.

"This morning," Sister Kawaguchi whispered in my ear. I could feel her hot breath on my temple.

"This morning Hiromi-san was once again detained."

I nodded. My geography book lay open to a red map of the Union of Soviet Socialist Republics. She turned the pages to a map of Turkey and tapped it with her pen.

"You will sit for one hour in front of the library tonight. And you will find no obstacles in your path tomorrow."

"Yes, Sensei. Thank you, Sensei," I said.

If only she knew what I did on those nights

out with Chiemi to make me so late in the mornings! I sat shivering at the thought of all my near misses; one evening, for example, when I was clearing a table at the kissaten, I looked down just in time to see Mr. Cockroach ascending the stairs. I ran behind the bar and crouched down out of sight. There was no need for me to explain to Maki who was behind it at the time, and she jerked her head at Chiemi to wait on the tables.

All six of the tables were full, so Mr. Cockroach sat right at the bar. Rolling my eyes upwards I could see the tips of his fingers over the edge of it and heard him order a coffee. I pressed myself against the pipes and valves of the sink, felt the cold water rushing through them as Maki discreetly cooled the cup before pouring Mr. Cockroach's coffee. I listened to the ugly clearing of his throat. He flicked open his lighter and lit a cigarette. Then he clicked the lighter closed. My calf muscles cried out in agony, and I squeezed my eyes shut. For half an hour he sat there at the bar, keeping me in bondage behind it. Then finally he got up, paid, and left. I fell on my hands and knees onto the rubber mat behind the bar. Maki sighed deeply, her hands on her hips, and then cleared away his fouled cup and dirty ashtray.

With my head full of ringing emptiness, I floated through the morning hours until lunchtime. Then I went outside to lean against the wall of the gym in the cold air. Along came my friend Mie Takayanagi wearing an irritable expression. She opened her bento and shoved it at me.

"Eat some of this," she demanded.

I looked at her lunch, the little black mass of hijiki like newborn snakes, and pressed my handkerchief to my lips. She narrowed her eyes at me and looked out across the tennis court. Her sinister profile made me want to laugh suddenly; the way she stood with all her weight on one foot, a tight fist on her hip, and the open bento in her other hand. A short laugh flew out of me, snatching back her attention. Mie's surname meant literally Tall Willow, and indeed she was tall. But she was much too sullen and funereal to be a willow. If she were a flower, she would have been a dark foxglove: shady, intricate, and poisonous. Mie hated school and its obstinate restraints, and at night in her room behind her father's old-fashioned sake shop, she threw off her school uniform and wrapped herself up in a black men's kimono. There she burned candles, and we lit our cigarettes off them and drank tepid sake from big rice bowls.

"Just have a little plain rice," she insisted, "or I'm ignoring you."

I shook my head. "I can't just now. I'll throw it right up for sure."

"You shouldn't drink so much," she said.

"I'm not," I told her, and she smiled a mean little smile like a grimace.

"Look then, do what you want, okay? But I don't even want to think about what might happen to you one day."

She closed her bento and wrapped it in its cloth untouched. Across the tennis court, Suzuki-Sensei was walking toward the administration building. Suddenly she slowed her pace and seemed to look straight at me.

"There's that new one," Mie said with annoyance. "What does she think she's looking at, anyway?"

Suzuki-Sensei turned away and kept going, and in my throat I suppressed a little agony of startled cries.

I was alone in the tiled hallway after everyone else, it seemed, had gone. As it grew dark outside, the rain turned to snow, and the wind whistled up and down the dim, empty corridors. Only the members of the various after-school clubs stayed late in isolated rooms. Behind the bare black cherry trees, the brightly illuminated convent stood guarded by the

121

stone statue of the virgin with her kabuki face. While nobody kept a watch on me, I knew that Sister Kawaguchi would feel it in her own legs if I stood up from my punishment too soon. So after exactly one hour, I hobbled outside and to the changing house, where I quickly put on my kendogi and went to stand at the wide open door to the dojo. Inside they were all in full combat, screaming out their meetings of the spirits and crashing their bamboo shinai onto each other. One of the second year sempai standing at the sideline caught sight of me and ran to the doorway, and I dropped to my knees and bowed to her.

"Please excuse me for being late!" I shouted, with my forehead almost touching the sill of the doorway. She gestured for me to go back outside and jumped out after me. I had been late far too often. I was late to school, and then thanks to that punishment I was late for the kendo club as well. I stood on the wet pavement in my bare feet. The snow was rapidly sticking and gathering, and I fought against shuddering as the muscles along my spine constricted violently.

"You stay outside until you hear the teacher call it quits," she said. "And kneel down." She started back in then suddenly spun around to face me. The light spilling out of the dojo illuminated part of her face inside the

mask like a swamp ghost from the movies.
"Tighten up," she said. "Make me see that you
aren't lost."

I thought I saw a little smile come and go
and then she flew back inside. I got down on
my knees with the snow falling all around me.

All along the wide boulevard the upstairs
cafes twinkled in the snow. I got off the bus in
front of Seibu department store and waded
into the winding streets of Sakanamachi.
Frozen and exhausted, I narrowed my eyes
against the blizzard. The little street I followed
became a hypnotic kaleidescope of flickering
neon tubing and shivering colored banners.
The big lanterns glowing outside the bars and
kissatens looked full of heat and magic, surrounded by furry pink light, and the lanterns
seemed to each house a benevolent demon,
promising laughter, love, and oblivion.

I forced myself up the stairs towards my
job, feeling as if I might just collapse before I
made it to the top. The blast of warm air when
I pushed open the door was almost shocking.
Chiemi nodded to me from behind the bar as
she poured whiskey into a cup of coffee. The
place was dim, warm, shimmering with the per-
fume of coffee and happy Django Reinhardt
music playing, and I felt a surge of relief flood
through me. I went into the tiny office to

change my clothes. As I put on lipstick and black mascara I could hear Maki's laugh. I tied on my apron and went out to the bar. All at once I felt the air being swallowed out of the room, and I fought for a breath with the sensation of sharp needles piercing my lungs. Standing at the bar with her hand on Maki's arm was Suzuki-Sensei.

Maki looked to me and smiled widely. She said cheerily, "This is my waitress, Hiromi." Clearly she hadn't been told anything and my mind went numb with confusion.

"Hiromi-chan," she continued, "This is my old friend Shiho, who I haven't seen in such a long time."

I forced a smile and imagined all of my teeth showing. The place was empty of customers except for two office ladies having whiskey-coffees at a table near the windows. They had on the pale uniforms of the Shiseido plant and were smoking cigarettes.

"We'll sit down and have a Marie Brizard," Maki said to me, and she took Suzuki-Sensei by the sleeve.

I carried their drinks over on a tray, while inwardly screaming. The little glasses knocked melodiously together as I dropped paper doilies onto the table.

"It really is freezing out, isn't it?" said Suzuki-Sensei. "Look, Maki-san, this girl's hands are trembling, and her cheeks are still red."

Maki looked at me. "So they are!" she said. "Hiromi-chan, have a Marie Brizard."

I shook my head. "No, thank you," I said. Suzuki-Sensei's unreadable, treacherous expression crowding together with the festive Django music suffocated me, and I turned away.

"What that kid likes is whiskey," I heard Maki telling her, and my anxiety fermented into a lush despair. The ladies from the Shiseido plant waved me down, tipsy on the coffees, and I went to face their maddening cheerfulness.

When Suzuki-Sensei had gone, after telling me effusively what an absolute pleasure it was to meet me, I collapsed into a chair at the bar. Maki looked sincerely concerned when she remarked that I did not look well, and I felt as if I might die soon. I felt almost hallucinatory, as if I'd taken belladonna. Chiemi poured me a glass of whiskey while Maki locked the door, and I swallowed it slowly, trying to hold the whiskey all around the raw, sore place in my throat. In my delirious state, the bar took on an ominous texture, and menacing shadows seemed to well up around Maki and Chiemi.

How could I possibly tell them who this Shiho was to me? I could hardly tell Maki that her old friend was probably at that moment planning my expulsion. It would only worry and embarrass her. I kept quiet and with my arms wrapped tightly around myself, I walked home through the snow-swirling entertainment district.

In my tiny room I fell into a feverish, tortured sleep and dreamed of being shamefully expelled. Dishonorably discharged back to Seattle. I dreamed of my mother all alone in her office at Nordstrom's and woke up nauseated.

During the geography lesson Sister Kawaguchi, with a raised eyebrow, gave me a summons to the pink infirmary. As I stood up to go out I looked over my class, 1-Bamboo, at all the pale necks and brushes of black hair bent over their colorful maps. Perhaps this is the last time I'll see this, I was thinking.

I pushed myself in the direction of my coming punishment, my throat feeling as if it had been burned and peeled. Once outside the door of the infirmary I stood paralyzed, drawing in great shuddering breaths of air, wanting to run as hard as I could, out through the high gates to Shijimizuka, down the winding road along the stone wall. I wanted to run all the way to the Nakatajima Dunes and drown myself in the winter ocean. I wanted to fall down and beg her, "Please don't ruin me, Shiho Suzuki!"

I knocked and entered the big room, empty but for her, looking up almost sadly from her papers.

"Come here and sit," she said.

I went to sit in the chair she indicated. Cold winter light came from the tall windows behind their bleached canvas curtains. The two beds looked as smooth as fields of untouched snow.

She looked at me, leaning on her desk and sighed.

"Suppose that it had not been me," she said. Her voice went through me like currents from a galvanic battery, and my throat tightened, but I dared not swallow into the raw pain of it. The pale colors of the room blurred all around Suzuki-Sensei's brown face and without difficulty, I found myself standing in the windy fields of the vast Mongolian grasslands. She rode up beside me on her mad, glad, frisky pony and smiled.

"Hiromi!"

I was yanked back to my cold chair and her focused black eyes.

"Listen to me! You know that you must quit that job. If I were another teacher, you would be getting expelled right now."

"How could there have been such a coincidence?" I whispered.

She slapped her open palm onto her desk. "It was no coincidence! I heard through the chain of my friends that Maki Ohta had a foreigner working for her so I went to see for myself. News like that is like a blown dandelion, and Sakanamachi is a small district." She narrowed her eyes. "You will eventually be discovered."

She reached out and pressed her hands against my face. They were like ice.

"Now look what a fever you have," she exclaimed, pushing her chair back. I watched her go to the little glass cabinet and come back shaking a thermometer. She unbuttoned my starched white uniform shirt, and a chill shuddered through me when she pushed the slick thermometer under my arm. Then she gave me some aspirin, and I forced the rough little pills up over the fiery mountain in my throat with the help of water from a pleated paper cup. Her hands rested on my bare shoulders, under the cloth, for a moment, and the great canvas curtains appeared to swell out before my eyes as if full of wind. The spirited drapes comforted me somehow as Suzuki-Sensei's admonishments began to rain down.

"You shouldn't be out at night wandering Sakanamachi in the sleet. You also shouldn't be drinking liquor! You might fool these old nuns, but you don't fool me at all!"

She looked at the thermometer and then pushed me towards one of the beds, jerking back the cover. "Get out of this," she said, pulling at my jumper. I let the jumper fall to the floor, wearing only my shirt, underwear and socks, and climbed into the bed, stunned by the firm luxuriousness of it. Her hand lay on my head and she said,

"You know, I am not so far away from you as you think. I am 25 years old." She massaged my neck and my shoulders, and I let my simmering eyes close. I was an underwater swimmer. The steam heat banged up through the pipes.

"And I was a bad girl once, too. Just like you."

I tried desperately to relax my muscles under her hands like healing vapors all around me. When she pressed her palms to my chest, I opened my eyes. The unfamiliar expression on her face panicked me, but she shook her head, and very suddenly she let go of me. Then I slept for awhile.

I remember being driven in her car to an austere clinic in a pine grove not far from the Nakatajima dunes, with Mie hunched up beside her in the front seat. I remember the cassette box on the floor, Yanagi George and Rainy Wood, and thinking, now I know something about her. She listens to Yanagi George and Rainy Wood on her way to school. The doctor at the clinic was stern and didn't talk to me at all. He spoke unpleasantly to Suzuki-Sensei while I sat half dressed on the examining table. Like a cat at a frosty veterinarian's office. He gave me a thick injection that hurt terribly as it forced its way into the vein. I didn't ask what it was. Then I was taken to Mie's house behind the sake shop, and Suzuki-Sensei gave Mie a bottle of pills.

"Let's keep this all quiet," she said, and Mie nodded.

When I woke up I felt much better, except for my right eye, which was swollen shut and teary almost as if I had been punched. In the bathroom I sat on the little wooden stool while Mie poured tubs of water over me. Then I sank into the deep hot bath and closed my left eye.

"Suzuki asked me an awful lot of annoying questions," Mie told me, crouching naked at the edge of the bath.

"Like what?"

"If we drink together ever, you and me. And I told her no, of course."

"Good," I said.

Mie's eyes darkened.

"You know, she's protecting you, but I don't like her one bit." She had on her angriest face.

"I get a very ugly feeling from her," she said, "a very ugly feeling."

On the TV that night Mie and I watched a black and white movie from the 1960s. It was a modern opera, but it had the feel of an old, old story. I forget now what it was called. I popped an antibiotic tablet with warm sake and leaned against Mie on the tatami. The movie opened at the funeral of an employee of a pharmaceutical company. His coffin had a rounded glass cover, and everyone at the funeral cried when they looked at him inside, as if sleeping, on a bed of white roses. He was not old. There was a dizzying series of flashy pill commercials for all the various medicines he had sold during his lifetime. "All those pills," sang-sobbed his wife at his coffin, "and they couldn't save him!"

Then the screen blackened, and I covered my bad eye with one hand. The dead man found himself in a deluxe apartment full of glitzy western style furniture. He passed his hands over himself in surprise, and sang of his confusion:

"My God ..." he sang in a soft voice, "I thought that I had died yet here I am..."

He lay down on the furry carpet splashed with shadow and light, and the camera moved close to his eyes, which darted about maniacally, glittering like the lights of a town at night in a deep valley. A woman, wearing a marvelous white kimono, materialized out of the light in his eyes. She seemed to slink along sideways without moving her feet, and her hands opened both beautifully and clawlike at once as she began to sing. Her face was powdery white, so that her eyes appeared as glittery black jewels, and her lips were mocking, lovely, and mesmerizing around her song, which she sang to the pharmaceutical salesman on the rug.

Her glossy hair was cut mod-style, and ominous music swelled around her. I thought of an old-fashioned Japanese horror tale set in what I imagined Las Vegas to be like.

"Oh, she's evil, that one," Mie said, lighting a cigarette. The beautiful temptress slithered to the man's side and produced a cigarette holder with a black cigarette in it from the sleeve of her kimono. Mie laughed. I thought that the woman was the most perfect creature I had ever seen, and the salesman sat bolt upright and stared at her.

"Who are you?" he sang to her, "What is this strange place in which I find myself quite alive and full of warm, pulsing blood?"

"I," she answered him in a sultry, smoky voice, "am capable of giving you life again. I am the mistress of reversed fortune, and I can send you back."

"Never have I seen such flawless beauty," he exclaimed, reaching out to touch her. She rose fluidly to her feet and turned away, her cigarette in one hand, the other running through her hair, revealing for a moment the ivory nape of her neck.

The salesman jumped to his feet and stood behind her, panting.

"If we come together," she sang cautiously, "you will add a year to what was already lived of your life."

She led him into a room taken up entirely with a vast luxurious bed.

"You must decide," she sang, sinking down onto the satiny sheets, "if that would be worth it."

"What the hell?" he sang recklessly, "If I'm dead now, what difference would it make after all?"

And they fell into an embrace on the bed, music coming up like wind through a long concrete tunnel.

Later the woman sat up, adjusting her mussed kimono and lighting another black cigarette in its holder. Then she vanished. When the man woke, he found himself alone. He listened to chimes in the emptiness all around him and looked down at the pair of silk pajamas he wore. He felt cold and wrapped his arms about himself. "Are you an apparition?" he cried, and the woman appeared to jell out of the puff of white steam that appeared when he spoke. This time she wore her hair up in a twist like Maki's.

"Oh, look out," Mie said. "You watch it, she's evil!"

The man began to laugh, rather insanely. She wore an exquisite, demonic expression as she pushed him to the floor. Then all at once she swooned and seemed almost innocent, sad, and troubled. Tears welled in her eyes and spilled onto the shiny table where sat crystal glasses filled with glistening liquid. Time passed in the movie, time indicated by the changing shades of the salesman's pajamas and the woman's coiffure. When she disappeared, he would wonder if she had ever been there and then suffer from eternal boredom. He wanted his old life back, his routines. He missed his long walk to the commuter train, crowds, baseball, his life.

He called out to her, and she appeared.

"I want to go back," he said, "I want you to send me back to my life."

She shook her head. "I don't think it is possible now."

"Why? You told me you could!"

She smiled dangerously and sang, "How old were you when you died?"

"Thirty-one," he sang, and she lit another cigarette. Exhaling she said,

"Well, we were together 54 times."

She took him by the hand and opened a sliding shoji screen. Behind it were the flames of an infinity of candles. They walked among them, and she explained,

"These candles are lives, they are all the lives in the world."

They stopped before a tall, barely burned candle with no flame.

"This one was a baby who suffocated," she said, "and this one," she went on, pointing to a candle halfway burned, "is a 48-year-old school teacher who lives in Gifu." They went on, and she showed him candles not lit at all, telling him,

"These are lives not yet begun. In here, you see, is every life past, present, and future. And this," she sang on, "is you."

His eyes widened with horror at the flame barely burning in a tiny pool of liquid wax. The taller flames all around it danced in his eyes, and he reached out and took the bit of scalding wax between his thumb and forefinger. It seared his skin and he cried out but dared not let go of it or shake the flame out. His hand trembling, he lifted his little flame to the untouched wick of a new, tall candle. At first it appeared to go out, and the man let out a lonely howl. A wicked smile crept across the woman's illuminated face, and she clasped her hands together. But then, darkly at first, a flame came up around the new wick, and the candle was alive. The screen went dark all around the evil temptress, shrugging off her defeat. Win a few, lose a few, she was thinking, most likely. We could hear the far off singing of the salesman, and then his head appeared upside down on the screen. I forget what he was saying, but there was the clear outline of a fetus around his head. Mie lit a cigarette on the short candle burning beside her. "This one's you," she said and blew it out.

While I slept that night, I took my burned feet to the mistress of reversed fortune in the infirmary. "If we are together, you add a dram of misery to your well of luck, and take one step closer to expulsion from this superb academic institution." She looked so much like Shiho Suzuki, and I shouted out, "Who needs institutions?"

I had hoped that I would have the courage to just not go near the infirmary at all. But as if in a trance I found myself there at noontime, bowing formally and apologizing for all the inconveniences I must have caused. Suzuki-Sensei stood in front of me with her hands on her hips. Big, veiny hands with long square fingers. Impulsively I reached out and touched one, and all at once she caught me by the chin, jerking my face toward hers.

"What's wrong with your eye?" she demanded.

Her angry voice and rough manner startled me and made me want to sob. She seemed not to have noticed my silly gesture and continued to study me sternly with my chin in her hand.

"I don't know," I stammered. "When I woke up, it just wouldn't open, that's all."

"All right, all right," she sighed, letting go of me as if giving up. She went and put the big teakettle on the ring and lit the gas with a whoosh. Then she told me to undress myself and lie on the bed. It seemed unnecessary, but still I did as she told me to. She prepared a tea-bag poultice and put it on my bad eye, then she massaged my temples. This time I was completely lucid and terribly self-conscious.

"Hiromi thinks she is invisible and indestructible, doesn't she?"

I didn't answer her.

"Listen to me. You have to watch yourself. You can't keep working for Maki. If you don't tell her, I'll do it myself."

She drew in a deep breath and sat beside me on the edge of the bed. Her hands rubbed my neck and then she lay them on my stomach. My entire body tensed painfully. I had the almost irrepressible urge to sit up and bite her.

"You don't know Maki. I do, and if you only knew how well! You have no idea. Maki likes to surround herself with pretty things, but she cares absolutely nothing about them. If they break, she just throws them away and gets new ones. Me, I've taken a risk for you. I've done it because I recognize you."

I took the tea bag away and opened my eye. When I looked at her, she just smiled.

Finally one night when Maki was out, I told Chiemi.

"You're lying!" she cried when I told her who Maki's friend Shiho really was. Chiemi's eyes grew wide and piercing and she dropped her dish towel onto the bar. Her voice fell to a whisper,

"She's a teacher at your school?"

In spite of my promise to myself, I went with Chiemi to Prison after closing the kissaten. The big red lantern with its black painted handcuffs swung in the chilly wind over the doorway as we entered. When we sat down in our usual place, the hostess brought us Uncle's bottle in its little coat.

"You so pretty, Pretty-pretty," she said huskily as she poured out our drinks. She winked at me.

Chiemi emptied her glass and poured another. "That hostess is really a man," she whispered. "Did you know that?"

When I woke up in my clothes on the bare tatami of my room, I had no memory of getting home. I forced myself into the bath and then into my wrinkled school uniform. When I reached shijimizuka, I stood outside the high wall and bent over in torment. I was more than an hour late. The thought of going through all the lateness punishments again was more than I could bear, and my reason spun uncontrollably away from me. Without hesitating, I slammed my bare fist into the rough stone wall. My head burst and my knees buckled, and I held my torn and trembling hand in front of me.

I went from the shoe room to the infirmary, creeping past the 1-Bamboo class where Sister Kawaguchi stood stiffly at the blackboard.

"Tell me again how you did this," Suzuki-Sensei said coldly.

She held my throbbing, bleeding hand in both of hers.

"I fell down on the way to school," I said, my voice little more than a whisper. She leaned close to me, her nostrils dilating, and said,

"And you fell on the back of your hand?" I nodded, my eyes on the big crying Christ.

"And that is why you are so late," she added. I nodded.

"Right," she said, pulling me to the sink.

"Hold out your hand here." She went to the table and returned with a bottle of rubbing alcohol. Then she opened it and poured its contents over my hand. I screamed as white hot-pain shot up my arm and convulsed my entire body, and she turned on the tap and shoved my hand roughly under the cold water.

"Don't lie to me, Hiromi," she said, her voice shaking. "Don't you ever lie to me." The faucet shrieked as she turned it off. She dried my hand with a towel and wordlessly wrapped a bandage around it.

"You see a big bar lantern and fly to it like an insect, don't you." She took me by the shoulders and shook me.

"I'm sorry," I said, and I was.

Miserable, I handed Sister Kawaguchi my excuse written in Suzuki-Sensei's quick, furious hand, and she examined my face through her bifocals. Her look affected me like biting a lemon. I caught Mie's alarming glare as I took my seat, and my wounded hand lay like a paw in my lap.

For several weeks, I did not go to Prison with Chiemi at all, and so I made it to school on time every day. I studied my reading and writing with Abe-Sensei, my special tutor, and in the dojo I whistled my shinai through the air

141

onto Big Tomoko's head as hard as I could, watching the whites of her eyes light up behind the slats of her mask.

Each time I went to the kissaten I hoped that I would have the strength to tell Maki I wanted to quit, but each time I said nothing.

One day the sky cleared, and I arrived at school unusually early. The damp air was full of rainbows, and I watched an old nun come out of the convent and walk slowly down the path carrying a big bowl of steaming water. As she bent to empty the bowl into the gutter, it slipped from her hands, the soapy water splashing up. She made a little hop backwards, and for an instant I saw a big crow in her place. Then she straightened up and examined the bowl to see if it had cracked. I found myself smiling. I started to the shoe room, but instead I followed the path around it, into the little snowy garden behind the infirmary. There stood Suzuki-Sensei at an open window, tying back the canvas curtain. I whistled to her, and she looked up, surprised. She stared out at me for a moment and then said,

"Hey you! I am not a dog, am I!" And she threw a pen out at me which hit me on the head. She laughed suddenly, the only time I ever heard her laugh, and closed the window. I reached down to pick up the pen, and as I started back to the shoe room, I thought I saw the greasy edge of Mr. Cockroach's shadow sliding around the corner, and a cloud floated over the sun.

That afternoon as I sat having lunch with Mie in the 1-Bamboo class, one of the third-year kendo sempai called out to me from the doorway. When I went to her, she pulled me out into the hallway.

"Hiromi," she said, examining me closely. "About Suzuki-Sensei, does she—well, has she ever touched you?"

My heart shrank. "Yes, of course she has," I said.

"No, I mean, has she ever touched you strangely?"

I shook my head. "Why?"

"Because," Yano-Sempai said quietly, "some of the others think she touched them strangely." Her eyes darkened.

"Well, not me." I said, and felt as if my well-being was spilling out all around my feet.

"All right, then," said the sempai, "but if she ever does, you tell one of us, understand?"

"I understand," I said, and I watched her take off down the hall filled with lunchtime chatter and laughter.

I went back in and sat beside Mie, who said, "So, what did she want?"

"Nothing," I snapped at her.

"Well," Mie shrugged, "She sure is ugly. That's for sure."

In the changing house, I told Eriko, Big Tomoko, and the others what Yano-Sempai had asked me.

"Hey, she asked me, too," said Eriko.

"Me, too," echoed two others.

"Not me," said Big Tomoko. "She didn't say anything to me!"

"Well, what does it mean?" I asked casually.

"Maybe she touched someone's bajaina?" Eriko offered, smiling.

"Did Suzuki-Sensei touch your bajaina?" she asked in an official voice.

"Not my bajaina!" Big Tomoko said and burst out laughing.

"Not my bajaina either," I said, laughing but troubled. I felt a deep, smoldering angst when I considered that Suzuki-Sensei might have done that to someone. And while I knew that she had not touched me that way exactly,

I also knew that somewhere in my laughter was a lie. Now I dared not go near the infirmary while Yano-Sempai was going around asking these questions. I laughed loudly with my friends while my heart slowed down and then stopped beating altogether.

I made every effort to not think about Suzuki-Sensei. But during small moments of unexpected calm, I would suddenly whisper her name, pressing the bruise to see if it still hurt, bringing waves of new suffering crashing over me. Finally when I could bear it no longer, I fabricated a sore muscle and went to the rosy infirmary. She had a brooding expression on her face when I sat down before her, telling her how I'd wrenched my shoulder in the dojo. I said it like an offering, and she didn't speak. She pulled her chair close to me and placed her hands on my shoulders. All the bitterness I'd had evaporated.

"Look, I'm really trying to behave myself," I told her, and her normally fierce eyes were full of sadness. But at that moment I saw only the absence of anger. I felt her lift her hands away, and the feathers of her breath at my temple. Then she took my ear in her cold fingers and caressed it, and by that little gesture I was nearly crushed with happiness.

"Right," she said abruptly, getting up.

"Undress yourself and lie down, and I'll massage you."

"But I don't need a massage," I said, wanting her only to talk to me, to hear me without the reprimands that always came with the massage. "Well then," she said, going to her desk and sitting down. Her face had lost all expression, and she murmured, "Go away. Get out."

I stood up and went to the door, expecting her to change her mind, to laugh at me. I wanted to tell her I thought she was crazy. But she sat at her desk with her forehead in one open palm, turned to the window away from me.

Nothing was ever said. It seemed that talk about Suzuki-Sensei was conspicuously absent. Every single girl at school seemed to be carrying around a black secret that only I wasn't let in on. The next time I set my blistered foot inside that room full of disinfectant and cotton, there sat Sister-White, unceremoniously returned. There was no sign that anyone else had ever inhabited the place at her little enamel desk where she sat reading.

"Hiromi-san!" she said, smiling warmly. "How very nice to see you!" I was dumbstruck. Sister White had gotten up and was coming towards me as if she might hug me. Of course, she didn't and just patted my cheek, saying,

146

"How are your feet?"

"My feet? Oh, well, my feet are fine," I said, and my eyes filled with tears.

"I just wanted to welcome you back, Sister."

"How kind of you," she said, visibly touched. "And I am very happy to be back."

I remember the day Suzuki-Sensei threw her pen at me. I would never have even considered whistling at another teacher. She was different. Had Mr. Cockroach been watching us that day? After she left, I had a pain in my chest. Things seemed drab even though it was spring. I almost asked Maki a hundred times about her, but I always stopped myself. After all, I had no valid reason to be interested. When I did by chance run into her one day, I was with Mie at the train station nearly a year later. I almost didn't recognize her, she looked so different.

"This is my husband," she said, and I looked at the ordinary man with her and smiled. Imagining all my teeth showing. She looked terrible to me; she looked exhausted. I wanted her to scold me for something, but she no longer had any reason to. She said goodbye, and she and her husband (husband!) were woven into the crowd. She had a lot of makeup on, awkwardly, like a bad disguise, and Mie said,

"She looked great! Didn't you think?"

And I agreed with her.

What could I possibly know of suffering, gladness, or love?

THE BURGLAR OF SHIJIMIZUKA

Just as the sky changed from black to violet, Mrs. Ikazuchi lay on her back with burning sticks of incense implanted in her skin like the quills of a porcupine. The aroma of this medicinal incense permeated the old house where she lived by herself, and apparently, it was the secret to her good health. After the incense, she would then eat one small tomato and some dried cuttlefish along with a cup of tea, before going to work in her illustrious garden. From her house above Akihasakashita, she could look out at the shimmering mountains illuminated in the many colors of first light; amethyst, lilac, apricot, orchid and gold.

Mie got the story from the sister of Mrs. Akojima, the one who was given the diary. Mrs. Akojima befriended Mrs. Ikazuchi in a strange way, and was taken into her confidence. At the time Mie told me this story, Mrs. Ikazuchi was more than one hundred years old, known to be the oldest living person in the city of Hamamatsu. She was the inspiration of several local and already famous songs, and most of the people who had remembered her as a young woman were long dead of old age themselves. But all who remembered the stories of her youth remembered a devastatingly beautiful creature who might have been completely insane.

Mrs. Ikazuchi was born during the Meiji era under the reign of Emperor Mutsuhito and without electricity. She was the eighth of eleven children in the Chikamatsu family, makers of Mulberrywood sewing boxes, whose entertainment was reciting poems aloud to one another while sitting around the kotatsu. She was the only daughter, and her parents called her Saeko. Even as an old lady, she had no use for television or other modern conveniences. She still lighted her house with spirit lamps and her bath was heated by coal fire.

Everyone knew of the beautiful fruit trees which flourished in the garden of Mrs. Ikazuchi. One of the local songs told of the garden where rain always fell and night never left, where the mad beauty held her black plums to the silver moon. The garden was always spoken of with a breath of fright, even when describing its beauty, which in fact almost nobody ever saw. Her house was one of the last remaining of the old fashioned architecture, built around its garden, in which after having her small breakfast, Mrs. Ikazuchi would spend the morning hours working.

The harvest of her garden she wrapped in pages of newsprint and gave away to her neighbors, all except for the tomatoes; those she ate herself. The plums from her trees she gave to young girls in sailor style uniforms riding their bicycles past her house on their way to Kaisei High School. The schoolgirls would see the little old lady in her gray linen kimono, bent over on her stick, clutching the parcel of plums out on the pavement in front of her house. They thought Mrs. Ikazuchi was an adorable creature, who always seemed to be smiling. (It was impossible to tell if she were really smiling or if it was just the way her face had settled around so many wrinkles, or if she were merely squinting in the gold-pink early morning sunlight.) She would stand and watch the girls riding past, and then all of a sudden she would wave one of them down, clatter out into the street, and press upon her the parcel of plums. She never said anything, but would bow her head shyly and turn away, hurrying back into the shadows of her house.

She had been a capricious and lovely child, and she grew into a famous beauty. The very first photographer in town took portraits of her which still hung in her house in their original frames. As a young woman she was discovered by a director of the flickers who wanted to put her in his romantic tragedies. But her parents refused, believing that the enigmatic world of shadow and light was unseemly. They had never seen a movie, but they knew what women in the pleasure industry were, and their daughter Saeko would have no part of it. She didn't counter her parents, but she was very disappointed.

There were many stories of men who had fallen in love with her, but the most provident of the stories told in sake bars was the one of Madame Matsushima, a beautiful society woman who had fallen terribly in love with Saeko. Madame Matsushima was the wife of a rich paper merchant and only a few years older than Saeko, who was just sixteen or seventeen herself. It was said that they became friends and would be seen in the flower gardens around the great castle, walking together with their heads bent beneath a janome umbrella in the gentle rain which in the stories was always lightly falling. Madame Matsushima had been to Paris and Venice with her husband, and from these foreign cities had brought splendid books and fabrics and prints, which she gave to Saeko as gifts. Then the story branched off in many directions; that the husband returned unexpectedly from a trip and discovered them together in a state of dishevelment, or that Saeko had simply refused to see her any more, unimpressed with her tales of foreign cities full of massive bridges and buttresses and verdigris spires. Madame Matsushima succumbed to a deep sadness which little by little took her health away. Recorded in public record is the suicide of Madame Matsushima, carried out with an obscure poison. This poison was said to have caused a terrible death, dissolving her inside and leaving her room in a shambles from her wretched fighting at the end. Whatever the reason, something had caused her to do it, and her suicide drove Saeko quietly mad.

In the district of Shijimizuka where Saeko lived, the houses were large and beautiful. Many of the estates of that epoch would later be destroyed by fire, and sat on the land where my school would one day be built by the Sisters of the Holy Names. Very few houses remained by the time I went to school there, where a wide, four-laned boulevard went past Kaisei High School in the direction of Nagoya. But around the time of Madame Matsushima's suicide, opulence blossomed in Shijimizuka.

All of the houses in the district began to

miss things; a pocket watch or a painting, sometimes just a fish from the kitchen. Then for awhile it was ladies' undergarments. The burglar would take every item of a lady's underwear in a house, leaving only an empty drawer. Many of the victims of the underwear thefts were too embarrassed to report them. There was a lady who lost her Tamo Chikamatsu sewing box in which she had hidden some love letters she wanted noone to see. Another said her diary had been stolen. She placed a notice in the paper to have it returned, and it was, with comments in the margins and certain passages crossed out. The handwriting was so beautiful, it was suspected for the first time that the burglar of Shijimizuka might not be a man.

Then abruptly, the burglaries stopped. Right around that time young Saeko was married off to Jiro Ikazuchi, one of the richest men in town. At 38, he was considerably older than Saeko, who was 19. He was soft and fleshy, and not at all handsome. In fact, he was horribly ugly. He also had a bad leg which he had to drag behind him and a twitch under one eye which made him appear to be constantly blinking. Saeko found him repulsive. She cried through the wedding ceremony, her white-powdered face streaked and her eyes red as blood.

Mie said that the Ikazuchis went to the spa at Hakone for their honeymoon, to take the mineral baths. Saeko had never seen such a magical place as the Turkish bath at the inn, with its tiled columns and bright mosaic walls. Beautiful creatures materialized and disappeared in clouds of white steam, immersed themselves in clear bluegreen water and spoke in quiet voices which echoed amidst the gentle and steady dripping, the crashing of waves from the attendant's buckets. She was shaken by the cry of a certain woman as the freezing water was poured over her, a cry of such tortured pleasure, that Saeko had to turn her head from where she floated to her neck in the hot pool. The woman was shockingly beautiful, and Saeko was lucky enough to look just in time to see her frown of agony and pleasure as it diminished.

While they were at the distinguished inn, a commotion erupted when a pearl was stolen from the rooms of a famous actress also staying there. She was called Kiku, and the pearl was in kept in a tiny pouch of red velvet on a string. Unless she got it back, Kiku would have to cancel all her performances. She had never gone before an audience without this pearl concealed somewhere in her costume.

Even though Kiku was almost thirty-five,

she was still a great beauty, and Mr. Ikazuchi
was a devoted fan. He offered to buy her another pearl, to even go himself to the peninsula
where the young women who could hold their
breath for five minutes dove down and found
them on the floor of the sea. But no other
pearl would work, Kiku told him, although she
was touched by the kindness of Ikazuchi and
his young wife. She began to have all her din-
ners with the couple, and Saeko sat quietly in
awe of the famous grand lady.

It was widely known that the actress had
recently lost her husband. He was an actor, and
had died in the middle of a performance. It was
said that when he died some people in the audience applauded because it was so dramatic. In
spite of her fame, Kiku had fallen into financial disarray. The lost pearl was her husband's
first gift to her, and provided a good excuse
now for accepting little gifts from Mr.
Ikazuchi.

It had become a quiet scandal that the
actress had become inseparable from the newly
married couple, with the husband much closer
in age to her than to his wife. Who couldn't
help but feel sorry for Saeko, gazing almost in
adoration at the older woman, oblivious to the
fact that her husband was ignoring her in favor
of the actress. They would have never guessed,

looking at the threesome having dinner together, that the lost pearl was right there, concealed
in the most intimate of hiding places all the
time. Perhaps when Kiku stroked the face of
young Saeko who sat shyly in the elegant din-
ing room of the inn, Saeko felt more vividly the
smooth presence of the pearl so well hidden.

After they returned home, letters would
come from Kiku addressed to Saeko. And
Saeko wrote back to her faithfully, sitting in
the garden with her little brush and ink, the
wind fluttering the thin paper. She would take
hours to write one letter. She was not pregnant
and her family began to worry. She had been
married for nearly eight months. She didn't
want to talk about it to her mother, who was
the one most concerned. Her mother thought
that if only she could get a glimpse at one of
the letters Saeko was writing to Kiku she
might know why. She bribed the postman to
bring her the next letter written to Kiku from
her daughter before it could be delivered.

Then the Ikazuchis made a trip to Kamakura to
see Kiku in a play. It would be her first performance without the pearl. Kiku had moved into
a beautiful house and invited the Ikazuchis to
stay with her. Her financial troubles seemed to
have calmed down considerably, of this the
lovely house at Kamakura was proof. The story

told was that one day Saeko found her husband in bed with Kiku and went wild with jealousy. She ran through the house like a hurricane, smashing Kiku's collection of theatrical dolls and musical instruments. Mr. Ikazuchi disappeared for a week, Saeko returned alone to Hamamatsu, and Kiku canceled the rest of her performances.

Soon after, the postman delivered to Saeko's mother a letter addressed to the actress, and opening it, Mrs. Chikamatsu read her daughter's anguished words: "you promised, you promised me. You promised it would only be money and words, but never that. How could you tolerate such a thing? I gave my heart away for nothing, it seems, and I cannot bear the pain of imagining you with my husband! I am ill from it, from the thought of his touching you. You have betrayed me and I have died a little death. I may be married to him, but he has never touched me."

Saeko's mother was overcome with pity for her daughter. No wonder she wasn't pregnant! Her own husband had never come near to her, so busy he was floating among red lanterns with whorish cabaret women. And to see such heartbreak in the letter! Apparently poor Saeko had already come to love her husband. Mrs. Chikamatsu sent her husband to have a private word with Mr. Ikazuchi, and that night

Saeko lay with tears rolling down the sides of her face in silence, her hands behind her head gripping her hard rice pillow. This way she became pregnant, and the commotion settled somewhat.

The robberies started again in the neighborhood of Shijimizuka, and more expensive things went missing. Jewelry and gold. The strange thing was that everything was always returned later by post, or left in a parcel somewhere outside the house from where it was stolen. Mrs. Ikazuchi had a daughter she named Hanako, and not long after, Mr. Ikazuchi's bloated body was pulled from the nearby canal. The doctors said that he had swallowed yaku, in its purest, most deadly form.

Hanako grew into an exact copy of her dead father. She was appallingly ugly with a wide nose like a snout, large nostrils and thick lips. Her eyes were tiny and close together, and her face was almost completely round. Even Saeko, her own mother, could see that her daughter was ugly. But in spite of her physical repulsiveness, she was a happy and clever child. This Saeko found heartbreaking, and she wished that such simple oblivion could be maintained forever. When Hanako was a student, Mrs. Ikazuchi would pick plums from the garden and wrap them in paper for her to take to school. Just as Saeko feared, Hanako was relentlessly teased by her classmates, and she hoped that if she gave everyone plums they would come around and like her. But it didn't happen that way. Hanako lived with her mother in the house until she died at 77, when Mrs. Ikazuchi was 98. She had never stopped treating Hanako as a child. Now she picked plums for the schoolgirls riding by.

When Mrs. Ikazuchi next broke into the house of a stranger, almost eighty years had passed since the last time she had done it. It was after Hanako's funeral. A flock of children followed the hearse, thumbs covered with their fingers. The old woman had always amused them with her sleight of hand, so that when she stopped in the street to play janken with them, there would always be something magically there when she opened her palm. A bright shell or a 100 yen silver. In her old age, Hanako had been adored by the children in the neighborhood, who couldn't tell the difference between what had once been lovely and once been hideous under all the wrinkles of the old mother and daughter.

On that day, after the funeral, Mrs. Ikazuchi took her dead daughter's shamisen into the garden and played it. Hanako had been very good at it, having spent her life learning, making up her own songs in the garden of fruit trees which would float up into the sky and hang in the evening mist. Mrs. Ikazuchi had knotted hands like little bonsai branches and she couldn't very well press the fine strings of the shamisen. But on that day she forced out a simple version of Sakura Sakura, sitting under the flowering plum.

When night fell, she went outside and started down the steep slope of the hill. She could hear the talking and laughing of televisions coming from the brilliantly lit houses, and the sounds of pots clattering and oil spitting in hot fry pans. Stopping at the gate of a darkened house she bent to read the name on the black plate bolted to the low concrete wall.

"A-KO-JI-MA" She read aloud.

She leaned on her stick with her chin in her fingers.

"Akojima ka," she thought aloud. "Well, I do not recall any such family in this part of Shizuoka prefecture," she murmured, opening the gate.

The house was not locked, and removing her wooden geta in the entrance way, she stepped up onto the tatami.

"Gomen Kudasai" she announced herself in a whisper, and then she laughed silently behind her hand. From her sleeve she brought out a wooden match and illuminated her way to the dark kitchen.

Light from the street lamp came in through the kitchen windows and Mrs. Ikazuchi went to the small refrigerator, which was decorated with a design of the Eiffel Tower. When she opened it, the room filled with light, and Mrs. Ikazuchi peered inside at the cans of Asahi beer, a jar of iridescent pickled ginger and beef-steak plant, anpan, a carton of miso paste, milk, eggs, film and lipstick.

"Arahh! What is this here," Mrs. Ikazuchi said picking up a black tube of Mary Quant lipstick. She opened it and examined the deep red color, then tucked it away into the sleeve of her kimono.

At that moment, Mr. and Mrs. Akojima came into the entrance way of the house, switching on the light. They noticed the small pair of wooden geta neatly placed on the tiles and looked at each other. They saw the glow of the refrigerator coming from the kitchen door-way. Standing at the open refrigerator, Mrs. Ikazuchi turned around in surprise when the kitchen was flooded with bright light, and found herself face to face with the young couple in evening wear and coats, a strange smile appearing on the face of the woman. Mrs. Ikazuchi tried to hide herself behind the kitchen table, blinking her eyes like a raccoon caught at the garbage in the sudden lights of a car. She must have been at least a hundred, so cute and sad, Mrs. Akojima was thinking, as she quietly walked toward the old lady with her hands outstretched.

Mrs. Ikazuchi found herself holding a cup of kukicha, sitting across the formica topped table from Mrs. Akojima. Mrs. Akojima was used to seeing Mrs. Ikazuchi as she left for work in the mornings, standing outside with her wrapped parcel. She had often stopped to watch the young girls passing, once she had seen the routine, and tried to guess which one the old woman would choose to stop. She had never guessed correctly, and supposed that it must have been completely random. Now she sat with her in the bright kitchen, somehow not surprised to have found her here. Her daughter had just died, after all, the poor woman, and she was probably senile at her age. Mrs. Akojima felt her heart aching with pity.

"You are very beautiful," Mrs. Ikazuchi said to her, her face crinkling into a smile. "You remind me of someone I knew long, long ago. But you are so tall! All of you girls nowadays are like giraffes, striding along with your heads in the sky. Not like when I was young."

Mrs. Akojima smiled. She tried to imagine

old Mrs. Ikazuchi young. She painted a picture in her head of a very proper young woman, whose world must have been so narrow compared to what hers was.

Then Mrs. Ikazuchi got to her feet and said she really had to go home. She liked to go to bed early and wake up before the sun. As she slipped on her geta at the door, which sat where she had left them when she entered the house as a burglar, she reached into her sleeve and brought out the lipstick. She handed it to Mrs. Akojima, whose eyes widened in surprise.

"I stole this but I would like to return it because you have been so kind to me," Mrs. Ikazuchi said. "And I'd like to invite you to come to my house tomorrow, if you would be so generous as to allow me that pleasure."

Mrs Akojima nodded and accepted. She held the lipstick in her hand. The old lady started towards the gate, then turned and said,

"I was once the burglar of Shijimizuka. They never knew who it was, or even got close. And it was me all along. Oh, those boring nights with nothing to do, how could I help it?"

She bowed very low at the gate and disappeared. Mrs. Akojima burst out laughing. She could hardly wait to visit the old lady.

Looking at the framed photographs of young Saeko, Mrs. Akojima was astounded. Not only had she been beautiful but full of wild spirits that hung all around her and filled her eyes with light. The way she stared out from behind the dusty glass was a dare, sultry, full of mischief and laughter. Like a beautiful tiger turned suddenly into a young woman. Mrs. Akojima turned to look at old Mrs. Ikazuchi, and thought aloud,

"This is you, you are this beautiful young girl!"

The old woman bowed her head shyly and waved a hand modestly. I wasn't so beautiful, her hand said. But Mrs. Akojima could hardly take her eyes from the photographs, so liquid and supple with life they were.

"Wait, I'll show you someone who was very beautiful," Mrs. Ikazuchi said, and she went to a cabinet and returned with a very old portfolio, tied with black ribbon crumbled with age. Inside were posters advertising old theatrical productions, all with the same actress called Kiku. Her hair was like lacquer and decorated with tiny umbrellas. In some she was dramatically made up, and the plays all had picturesque titles; The Wandering Smoke Flower, The Drowned Hyacinth, Laughing Ghosts in the Lamp, The Song of the Magic Water, The Dragon Maiden.

"You knew her?" Mrs. Akojima asked.

"I knew her very well once," said Mrs. Ikazuchi. "From more than eighty years ago, I knew her."

Mrs. Ikazuchi ran her fingers lightly over the brightly colored posters. What a wonderful design sense they had then, Mrs. Akojima was thinking. The posters were probably worth a fortune.

"She was my secret friend for many years after my husband died."

Mrs. Akojima caught the scent of the medicinal incense around old Mrs. Ikazuchi's voice.

"She would have to come in the absolute dead of night to visit me. I don't think anyone ever caught on, but people sense things, they do. Just the way they never knew that I was the burglar, but they felt something about me, this I know. And how they talked about the Burglar of Shijimizuka, as if it were so frightening! I returned everything I ever stole after all! Well, except for the fish. You can't really return that in all fairness."

Mrs. Ikazuchi chuckled. As they sat in the unused sitting room of the old house, the late afternoon sunlight slanting in through the parted ancient shoji screens, Mrs. Akojima looked at the millions of tiny dust particles in the light like the beam of a movie projector. She gazed at the lovely, almost sinister face of the long ago actress, lost forever to the disinterest of the modern world, while the spirited, frisky young Saeko looked down from her frame.

Old Mrs. Ikazuchi lit a spirit lamp and heated water for her tea. The moon was nearly full, spilling its pale light over her garden. A few houses away Mr. Akojima sat in front of the TV eating a hamburger. He got up and went to the kitchen. "Do you want a beer?" he called out. He was a good husband. But Mrs. Akojima was lost on the couch with the diary Mrs. Ikazuchi had almost begged her to take and read. By opening the thick black book with its ancient pages of transparent rice paper Mrs. Akojima had fallen into another world. She breathed the steamclouds of the Turkish bath at Hakone, where Saeko was carefully pushing into herself the smooth pearl and all its applause. What spunk the girl had, slipping into the actress's room and watching her sleep. The gentle rise and fall of her bare breast partly visible, her open hand. So what if she got caught, what was the worst that could happen? Saeko leaned closer and closer, until she could feel Kiku's soft breath against her own lips. Kiku moaned in her sleep, and Saeko pulled back. She crept toward the door, noticing on the tatami beside the folded fan and handkerchief, the little velvet pouch..

One day Mrs. Akojima went to visit old Mrs. Ikazuchi in her garden. Mrs. Ikazuchi was picking cherries. "Have anything you like," she said to Mrs. Akojima.

Beneath the outline of the old lady, Mrs. Akojima could see Saeko, taunting her. This old lady had climbed windbent pines to the rooftops of some of the richest houses in the district. She had played with their underclothes and jewelry, read their diaries, and had laughed wildly inside at the ridiculous police. She had met Kiku at the gate in the moonless blackness, Kiku holding her lacquered wooden geta in her hand in order to slip quietly through the streets in her stockings. Mrs. Akojima felt her eyes wanting to rest against the image of Saeko the way she looked in the old pictures. We wouldn't even speak, just smile with such crazy happiness, and our smiles were just silent laughter. And then I would pull her down and in the dark place near the entrance to my garden find her breast beneath the layers of cloth. I could bite her if I wanted to, she allowed that, but I was always having to listen carefully in case Hanako would wake up.

"I've had the most boring, uneventful life imaginable," Mrs. Akojima wanted to say. "Why would you ever be interested in me?"

"Ne, ne!" Mrs. Ikazuchi called out to her again, "Have anything you like!"

"I'd love a plum," Mrs. Akojima said, and to her surprise the old lady cried out, "No! NO! any other thing, but not the plums!"

Seeing the shock on Mrs. Akojima's face she quickly explained,

"You are beautiful, you see? I only give the plums to ugly girls."

She dropped a cherry into Mrs. Akojima's hand, and Mrs Akojima marveled at the way the deep line between Mrs. Ikazuchi's nose and chin unfolded a smile. A little clap of thunder startled a flock of tiny birds resting in the branches of the plum trees, which spiraled into the sky and off in the direction of the pale mountains.

THE SUBCONSCIOUS MUSEUM

Mikayo had pulled the buckles of her canvas corset so tightly about me that walking
along the narrow street with the diabolical sun
lashing down, only the most shallow breaths
were manageable. With each step I was assailed
by a small electrocution which subsided with
strange shimmering waves of pleasure, wringing the juices from me as I went to buy the
tangerines Mikayo had asked me for. In my
curiously aroused temperament I considered
the odd enchantment of our ethereal friendship. It felt momentous, saturated with ebul-
lient spirits.

I started across the Sato bridge which arched
up over the canal. A bus went thundering past and
I was momentarily choked and blinded by the cloud
of fine dust and poisonous vapours it left behind.

I tried to cough gently. The very drawing in of breath was at once punishing and rapturous. On the still green water of the canal slender seabirds drifted among the long weeds floating on the surface like veins. I could feel the sweat running down my sides inside the stiff canvas, and a tremor passed through me when I imagined Mikayo herself sweating in it, and the fabric of the white corset with its buckles of stainless steel having recorded in moisture all of her torturous suffering and disappointments.

The fruitseller's low awning was covered with green grasshoppers. Their gold eyes watched me as I stepped beneath it into the cool, dripping fruit shop. My eyes adjusted quickly to the dim light and I bent over a bushel of tangerines. As I did, my ribs were crushed inward, sending a bright flash of pain through my upper body and straightening me up again. I stood amidst the bushels of pears and melons and mangoes breathing carefully for a few moments. Then I looked again at the tangerines, each one wrapped in delicate red paper, and thought of Mikayo lying on her futon beside the fan and a mosquito coil in the upstairs bedroom. I bent again over the tangerines and filled a paper sack. Later I would find little blue bruises on my abdomen which the corset had marked me with and press them lightly with my fingertips.

When I joined the kendo-bu, Mikayo Yamazaki was made my special instructor by Koizumi-Sensei, our teacher. She had very bad asthma, but still she had the highest degree of any of the third year sempai. I remember her dropping down and taking hold of my bare ankles to position my feet the way she wanted. "Like this," she said, jumping up again. "Position your shinai a bit lower, and bounce a little more on your feet, like this." She hopped lightly back and forth and then brought her shinai down on my head. I could see her eyes shining inside her mask. She was like a wild-flower.

I had seen Koizumi-Sensei on his knees, his blue-black hakama spread out around him on the floor, frantically tearing off her mask when the asthma took all her breath away. I saw him carry her in his arms and run down the long drafty hallway to the infirmary, with her damp hair sticking to her forehead and her lips gone blue. I remember her face upside down, her eyes partly open and rolled back in her head, and the bruised-looking skin around them. The sound of Koizumi-Sensei's bare feet pounding against the wooden floorboards of the corridor, and Fujitani-Sempai clapping her hands together and shouting at us to fall into lines and sit. But that was only once. What I

remember more clearly was the sight of
Mikayo-Sempai removing her mask and
unwrapping the blue and white cloth from her
head. I marveled at the perfect shaft of late
afternoon sunlight streaming in on her as she
shook her head, little drops of glistening sweat
falling away from her like rain.

On the day Koizumi-Sensei sat before us in
the dojo and told us what had happened to her,
I looked at Big Tomoko's ears turning red in
front of me and listened to the startled breaths
and whispers all around me. The second and
third year sempai all sat solemnly along the
opposite wall from us. Fujitani-Sempai, the
one who looked like a boy, had her hands
pressed to her lips and her eyes were full of
tears. Even Ishikawa-Sempai, the meanest
one, looked stricken and I found myself wish-
ing it had been her instead, why couldn't it
have been her instead?

Earlier in the day I had caught sight of
Ishikawa-Sempai's sullen face as I passed the
second year bamboo class. Daly-Sensei, the
English teacher was leading them in a vocal
exercise. "Repeat Ahftah me," I heard her say
in her tight manner, and I had slowed to listen.
"Oh dear, what can the matter be?" she started, and then the class followed in its impossible Japanese accent, "Oh deeya, whatsu canza
matta bee". I had continued down the corridor

as Daly-Sensei finished; "Three old ladies stuck in the lavatry; they were there from Monday till Saturday; not a soul knew they were there!" I laughed aloud into my hand at the familiar rhyme I had heard Daly-Sensei repeat so many times. Now the words rang in my head like glass as I watched Fujitani-Sempai get up silently and go to the big door of the dojo. It had rained, and when she slid open the door a damp mossy breeze floated in. A "Soul", Daly-Sensei had explained, can merely be a person.

Somebody had found Mikayo-Sempai curled up in the entryway to her house, with her keys beside her on the tiles. Her shoes were mysteriously absent and she had wrapped herself in the pages of the Mainichi Shimbun. She was the color of ripe plums. The only thing she knew for sure, Mikayo-sempai had said to the police, was that she had been lying in the entryway from Saturday night, and it was Monday when the neighbor found her.

Listening to the story, I bit down on my tongue until tears came to my eyes. Once, not long after I had joined Kendo-bu I saw Mikayo-Sempai in town, approaching from a distance on a little street full of teashops. She was alone, wearing her school uniform even though it was Sunday. She saw me, too, and when she was close to me I suddenly looked away and kept walking. I horrified myself by doing that, by not bowing and greeting her as was expected, and I suffered over it, imagining what she must have thought of me. Ignoring a Sempai was a punishable offense, and at the very least, I would have to offer her a formal apology.

The following day, after school cleanup, I saw her as I went along the path to the dojo. She was standing near the chapel with two of her friends, laughing with them. She had her hand over her mouth, and one of the two girls with her bent forward and said something. They all doubled over again laughing. I stopped behind a small pine tree and watched them for a moment. Then I went on to the dojo and to the small changing house behind it. Only Big Tomoko was already there, changing into her Kendo-gi. It was her turn to make tea for the older girls. She disappeared into the little room which served both as a laundry and kitchen to put the kettle on.

When I went into the dojo Mikayo-Sempai was there, her perfectly pressed hakama swishing as she walked back and forth before the big mirrors on one wall. I went to sit before her and said,

"Sempai, I am sorry I did not greet you yesterday."

I glanced up at her. Her face was very serious, with no trace of the laughter I had seen before with her friends. She crouched down on her haunches facing me.

"Was your tongue tied?" she asked me seriously. I nodded my head.

"Well, alright, stick it out and let's look at it," she said. Her eyes were bright.

"Go on, stick your tongue out," she said.

I pushed the tip of my tongue out between my lips and closed my eyes.

"Farther, all the way," Mikayo-Sempai urged me. I pushed it out and she took hold of it between her thumb and forefinger and pinched it. Then she shook it a little until it hurt, and I saw that she was smiling. She let go.

"Okay? Now it's all untied," she said, still smiling. For the entire practice I had the taste of hand cream in my mouth.

Several times when I went to the infirmary to have Sister White bandage my feet I had seen shocking things. Once there was a girl lying in one of the beds who twitched violently every few minutes, then lay still again for awhile until the next twitch. As Sister White wrapped my feet, I sat in a chair and watched the twitching girl from the corner of my eye. I wondered what could possibly be wrong with her, since Sister White didn't seem the least bit concerned.

When I returned to the changing room later that day, everyone was excited and shouting. Big Tomoko told me that one of the second year archery students had been shot with an arrow in the meadow behind the school. It was only a flesh would, but it had bled and bled until the girl had turned completely white. At first I thought that the girl I had seen in the infirmary had been her, but in fact the twitching girl turned out to be the one who shot the arrow.

Another day I saw a girl sitting in a chair with Sister White and Sister Mochizuki bending over her, and I saw that a trickle of blood, like a tear, was coming from her eye. The room was full of abnormal sorrows. It was when I saw the girl crying blood that I learned better than to ask questions.

It was October when they found Mikayo-Sempai. She told the female police officer that she was cold and hurting. I could not imagine her saying that. In the ambulance a police officer offered a white-gloved hand but Mikayo said, "Oh, it's all right, I'm okay now."

Her injuries made a long list, many fractures along her spine, broken ribs, a collapsed lung, a broken foot. Perhaps she had been run over by a vehicle of some sort, the doctors told her mother, who only wore formal kimonos. Whatever it had been, Mrs. Yamazaki said, it was her fault for not having been there, for leaving Mikayo alone for a weekend. She would eliminate any luxury from her own life as punishment for this negligence.

At first when I went with Big Tomoko and the first year kendo-bu to the hospital, we took turns two at a time to sit with Mikayo-Sempai. She was kept tranquilized after they opened her and rebuilt her inside. She was delirious, and kept saying that her doctors studied the buttresses of medieval European cathedrals in order to reconstruct her. Big Tomoko and I sat at the foot of her bed in our drab wool overcoats decorated with the school insignia. I looked at Mikayo's tranquil face in the subdued winter light, and at the window, where outside the snow was gently and silently falling.

"You know," Big Tomoko said on the bus going home, "if that had happened to her a month later than it did, she would have certainly frozen to death."

A clear picture of Mikayo-Sempai dead in the tiled entryway formed in my mind like a memory. I pictured the neighbor who found her, an elderly lady in dark linen, running back and forth in fright and confusion, the long fabric of her kimono sleeves like wings flapping in the icy wind. Then I imagined Mrs. Yamazaki. What her screams would have sounded like! The gears of the bus ground loudly as we began the ascent toward Akihasakashita, and I stared past Big Tomoko beside me at the lights of twinkling houses rushing past. My imagination swarmed with an unwelcome mayhem of shouting voices. It seemed that every sigh and scream and whimper that would have been uttered had she been dead in the entryway welled up at once in my ears, twisting me arduously this way and that on the soft velvet seat of the bus. For a moment I was afraid that I might start screaming myself, when the sudden illuminated majesty of Hamamatsu Castle covered in snow quietened the commotion in my head.

Mikayo would have to lie still for a long time. Her bruises faded little by little, and she was the pale lily again that she had been, but she seemed less formidable. Mrs. Yamazaki brought bags of prepared food from the market in the basement of Seibu department store. The hospital room was stacked with neatly folded shopping bags with the same green and blue circles.

"Mom, I can't eat all this," Mikayo said with annoyance in her voice. "Take some of it home."

Mrs. Yamazaki threw up her hands. I looked at the willows decorating her bright obi as she moved back and forth.

"The problem is that you do not eat enough, Mika-chan, not that I buy too much. And the food here is atrocious. Can you honestly tell me that you would prefer to eat what they give you in this hospital? Watered-down miso and poached cuttlefish?"

Big Tomoko looked at me with her eyes glistening and laughing.

Because of the lateness of kendo practice and my secret parttime job, it was difficult to visit Mikayo in the hospital very often. But one Sunday evening I went alone to see her. When I entered her room I found her lying all by herself, illuminated blue by the flickering television. Her hair was damp as if just recently washed, her eyes sleepy and unnaturally serene. I had a fleeting impulse to climb upon her bed and wrap myself around her. I could almost feel the damp skin of her forehead against my cheek and smell the minty hospital soap. I bowed to her and greeted her formally before I sat down in the chair beside her. Mikayo-Sempai started to laugh, lightly at first, then more hysterically, shaking her head from side to side. I wanted to look over my shoulder or into a mirror, but I sat still until her laughter had subsided. She waved her hand dismissively in the air.

"I've gone a little mad lying here," she said. "My mother is driving me insane. Do you know what she brought today?" She raised her eyebrows at me.

"She brought live lobsters wrapped in a furoshiki. And I don't even like lobster. She wanted the hospital kitchen to cook them, and they wouldn't, so she got very angry and sulked out in the hall for hours. She only just left now."

Her eyes closed and I watched her pale face change colors in the television light. Disinfectant saturated the air in the room. I could have reached out and touched her sad, quiet face, petted her. I was consumed with a curiosity, the way I might have been if faced with the opportunity to caress a tranquilized wild animal. But my hands stayed pressed together on my knees as I listened to her breathing. A sinuous misery swam in a continuous circle over the bed where she lay, and like a serpent, it paused in its furrow over her head to stare at me with its yellow eyes. I'll do anything for you, I thought, looking at her.

She opened her eyes and looked at me placidly. "Well that's kind of you," she said.

"Don't be so formal, that is what I'd like. Just be normal."

At the very edge of sleep I could sometimes feel her presence in my room as if she were there. I know you are here, I would think, can you feel me knowing? I dared not go alone too often to see her for fear of calling attention to myself. But even when I did, her mother was almost always there, each time wearing a different magnificent kimono. And Mrs. Yamazaki's demeanor filled the room so completely that there was almost no air left to breath for anyone else whenever she was there. She busied herself turning the pillows, folding blankets, opening and closing the windows, all the while scolding Mikayo for everything from not eating to not complaining sooner about the volume on the TV. Mikayo's father had owned one of the best kimono shops in the city, which had been in his family for almost 100 years. Since he had died ten years before, Mrs. Yamazaki had run the business herself with relentless precision, the way she seemed to do everything.

One day when I arrived at the hospital, she was standing in the room wearing a dazzling black and green kimono. It was her white obi which caught my eye, arrestingly decorated with a twisting salmon in deep reds, golds and greens. It had bright yellow eyes, and while Mrs. Yamazaki paced back and forth at the foot of her daughter's bed, completely ignoring my presence in the room, the eyes of the salmon never left me.

As I was about to leave, Fujitani-Sempai came breathlessly into the room, wearing blue-jeans and a bugs bunny sweatshirt. I had never before seen her in anything but her school uniform or kendo-gi, and when I bowed to her my eyes pulled away from the floor to sweep her over from head to toe. She was one of the most strict of the third year sempai, humorless and assiduous. But among the girls in my level she had by far the most fans because she was tall and lean. She looked like a beautiful boy, she was kakkoii beyond imagining. I had seen girls in the first year changing room crying because Fujitani-Sempai had not looked at them when they greeted her. I had heard more than one say 'I love her' through her tears, and the stronger ones just laughed and made plans on how to soften Fujitani-Sempai's solid heart.

I looked at her serious face as she stood beside the bed. Mikayo-Sempai waved her hand at her and said, "Oh, Chiaki-san, how are you?"

Mrs. Yamazaki instantly became noticeably irritated. She smiled tightly at Fujitani-Sempai and said,

"You really should not have made this long trip just to come for a short visit," she said to her. "You are far too kind, and I'm sure that Mikayo feels very sorry that you have had to inconvenience yourself so."

I looked at Mikayo-Sempai's face. She had made it completely blank, a trick I had started to recognize. Mrs. Yamazaki turned to Mikayo and said, "Mika-chan, I am going to get some tea."

She went out, and even though I had only just arrived a few minutes before, I found an easy excuse to leave.

I glanced back through the door from the hall. I could see most of Mikayo-Sempai's bed, her hands and wrists which disappeared suddenly, and Fujitani-Sempai's bag on the floor near the door. I could almost feel Fujitani-Sempai leaning over the bed. And there was complete silence coming from the room. On the way out I passed the cafeteria where sat Mrs. Yamazaki in perfect posture, with an angry expression and a cigarette held delicately between her fingers.

One Saturday, having washed the kendo-gi of the older girls in the big tub over the fire in the little kitchen, I was wringing them out behind the changing house when I heard a strange laughter coming from the dojo. It was late in the afternoon, and most everyone had gone home. Had it not been my turn to do the laundering, I would not have been there either. I paused a moment, bending over the twisted garment in my hands, to listen. There was nothing, so I carried an armload of the soaked gi out along the path through the flower garden to the clothes line which was strung between two pine trees behind the chapel.

When I returned to the kitchen and started to gather more into my arms, I again heard a cackle floating from the direction of the dojo. This time I thought I also heard a sob. I wiped my hands on my gym jacket and went to peek through the big open doorway. Ishikawa-Sempai and Watanabe-Sempai stood with their hands on their hips over Big Tomoko, wearing only her bra and underpants crouched on the floor. Her face was bright red like a beet, and I could see Ishikawa-Sempai's gleaming white teeth.

"Get up!" Watanabe-Sempai said firmly.

Big Tomoko didn't move, but wrapped her arms around herself. I saw her red eyes look up at them pitifully.

"Please, don't make me do this," she said quietly.

"What, make tea? You have to," Ishikawa-

186

Sempai barked.

Big Tomoko's gym-suit lay in a pile beside her.

To make tea, she would have to go outside and several yards into the first year changing house to the kitchen. And she could be seen from the tennis court, where several of the ten-nisu-bu still practiced.

The cackle flew out of Ishikawa-Sempai and hovered scurrilously in the air around her head. Deep crimson shame emanated from Big Tomoko, whose dimpled thighs and large breasts she tried vainly to shield with her arms. She stood up slowly, not taking her eyes from the floor. I pulled quickly away from the door-way as Ishikawa-Sempai started to turn in my direction.

Quickly I ran on my bare feet to the corner of the dojo, and peeked around as Big Tomoko, hiding her face in her hands rushed from the open doorway in her underwear. She almost flew over the short path into the changing house, and my heart fluttered with relief when she had disappeared inside. On the narrow vis-ible stripe of the tennis court I could see noone. Big Tomoko had been lucky, noone had seen, but since she didn't know this, she might as well have been seen by the entire school. Two peels of laughter rang out from the dojo.

"Yuriko, you have a heart of lead," snickered Ishikawa-Sempai's voice.

"Me!" Watanabe-Sempai laughed. "You started it, the 'make tea in your panties' game. You have a heart of ice and the mind of a snake."

I hurried back to the changing house, where my pile of wet washing still sat on the table beside the hotplate where Big Tomoko stood sobbing at the kettle. She turned and looked at me with distorted lips and bloody eyes. An image of her smiling, broad face passed behind my eyes, of her handing me a little package from the handkerchief shop. "It has Kenji Sawada's picture on it!" she was saying, "I got one for everybody."

She looked back at the tea kettle, and the tray with the blue ceramic pot and two teacups. I rested my hands on the pile of wet gi, then quickly gathered up as many as I could and ran to the line. The ones I'd already hung were swollen with breeze, and I strung the rest up alongside them. On my way back, I saw Sister White chasing after a bright green tennis ball and I hurried my step and caught up with her.

"Sister," I panted, and she looked at me affably.

"What is it, Hiromi-san?"

"I have a strange spot on my thigh, it hurts. Can you come and look at it?"

She frowned.

"Now? Can't you come after I've finished with the tennis practice?"

My heart beat haphazardly like a trapped bird's wings.

"Well, it's also bleeding too, and it is a funny color."

Sister White's hand holding the tennis ball dropped to her side, and she rested all her weight on one foot. Her lips pursed and she said,

"I see. And this thing on your thigh, is it also singing?"

I glanced at the tennis court, where the girls had continued practicing without her.

"Yes," I said, "it is singing as well."

Sister White followed me to the changing hut, where Big Tomoko was just pouring the water into the teapot.

Sister White took one look at her in her underwear and looked quickly away. Big Tomoko gave a little shriek, and Sister White chuckled.

"This is a very casual little house today," she said, sitting down on one of the benches.

"Hiromi-san, why don't you serve the older girls their tea so this poor girl can have time to change."

I carried the tray into the dojo. Ishikawa-Sempai and Watanabe-Sempai were sitting on the floor in their uniforms and jackets. A sharp look of annoyance came over Ishikawa-Sempai's face when she saw me.

"Excuse me," I said, and I lay the tray on the floor beside them.

"Where is Tomoko?" she snapped.

"She is still inside the changing house," I answered her.

I listened to her feet run across the floor to the door, and then to her sudden, obsequious voice in all its politeness greeting Sister White.

Later on, as I walked along with Big Tomoko, water and white soap foam rushed through the storm gutter beside the sheer stone wall. We had to shout over the torrent winding down the circuitous road, and the disparagement began to recede from Big Tomoko's face. She was not a weakling, and she seemed to have forgotten that anything adverse had just taken place. We walked all the way into town, along the wide boulevard through the city center, with its sand-colored marble sidewalks. Big Tomoko pulled me into Ikeya records, and I heard her untroubled voice asking the clerk, "Do you have the new Mayumi Itsuwa tape?"

I was reminded of that day as I walked along a narrow street in Mikayo's unfamiliar district, bound into the tight corset for the first time, beside a flooding storm gutter which drowned all the sounds around me. She had tightened it as tightly as it would possibly go, objecting all the time that it must be far too much for me. Yet I could see as I knelt on the tatami beside her bed, that she was pleased when I said, "No, make it tighter still."

Once she was brought home to convalesce, her mother returned to work again, and left Mikayo by herself since she was allowed to move around while wearing the corset. The house was two-storied, and extremely tasteful, furnished with very old and fine Japanese-style furniture. The bathroom was especially lovely, all wood like the ones in the most expensive antique inns, its marvelous deep bath lined with copper. Mikayo took the large upstairs room of her older Sister who had moved away, because it had the advantage of having its own toilet and big windows affording a nice view of the trees and the little garden below. Her house was much closer to the school than the hospital had been, and I went to see her as often as I could.

She could look like a child to me for a moment, and then she would move, or speak and she was suddenly much older than I was again, older than her actual three year advantage. The pills in the hospital had made her languid and fearless. She had looked angelic almost, as if she were always on the verge of dying. Months later, at home, when her spine had finally fused with the bones borrowed from her hip, she could manage short walks outside wearing the curative brace. Without the narcotic, she was tortured by pains everywhere and wondered if it was her spine or the stiff white corset itself that caused the aches and burns she felt. Only when she would take the corset off and lie still on her back, or when she had a bath, did she have some relief.

It was after she showed me her scars that I began wearing the corset whenever I went to see her, always when her mother was out. She did not like the scar along the length of the spine. She could never again play kendo. The scar which I wanted to touch was the one at her side, with the length and thickness of a wooden match, where they opened her to reinflate her fallen lung. I imagined her asleep on a shiny metal table, her face the way it looked after the asthma attack, damp and beautiful, like death. And the glossy-haired, immaculate doctor pressing his lips to the incision in her side and blowing air into her like a rubber toy. I wanted to put my own lips against it, to rub it with the tips of my fingers.

She was in such pain, and had asked me to help her in the bath. She sat naked and unself-conscious on the wooden stool while I sprayed her with the hand-shower. I held on to one of her hands, letting my other hand brush the scar under her ribs. Then I took both of her hands in mine, and as I helped her into the bath, only the twisted expression of pure discomfort on her face kept me from really looking at her body. I sat beside her and watched her face finally relaxing.

"Can I wear this thing?" I asked her, holding the corset, when she lay back down after the bath. And she had regarded me with interest.

"Why?"

"So I can feel the way you feel," I said.

After Big Tomoko had bought the new Mayumi Itsuwa tape and gone home that evening, I went to the hospital on the bus.

When I arrived, I found not only an agitated Mrs. Yamazaki, but also Fujitani-Sempai with a tormented look on her face. Both were in the hallway outside Mikayo's room, and I quickly turned away and went to sit on a bench in the waiting room. I watched as Fujitani-Sempai passed by and went out the double doors, and I thought I saw a tear glistening at the corner of her eye. After a torturous wait, I watched Mrs. Yamazaki also pass by and go out. The visiting period would soon be over, and I hurried to Mikayo's room. She had been crying and her face was streaked and pale. I faltered when I saw her and mumbled an apology. My embarrassment filled me with unnatural heat.

"No, don't apologize," she said, and I sat down. "I can't study," she said, looking at the ceiling.

"I can't do anything at all, my head is full of cotton. I can't study for the college exams." She looked at me and I saw a tiger's face.

"My mother told me that she thinks whatever happened to me happened because of a flaw in the way I think. In the way that I am. She was very angry today, almost insane. And she told Chiaki—Fujitani—not to come anymore. She told her she is a distraction to me. She doesn't like Chiaki."

"But why?"

I thought of Fujitani-Sempai and her diligence. She was always the first there in the morning at the early practice, and the last to leave at night. She had won awards for academic excellence.

"Because I used to love her," Mikayo-Sempai had said, looking toward the window where the sun had turned a deep red.

I didn't ask her any more questions. I knew better, that a question like the ones pounding the inside of my head were the type which could bring tears of blood. So I told her what had happened to Big Tomoko, about the lesson in humility from Ishikawa-Sempai. A mist clouded Mikayo-Sempai's eyes, and then a strange smile came and went. She shook her head.

"Don't think about it anymore," she said, "It will be all right."

The following day when I entered the dojo I found Ishikawa-Sempai sitting on the damp ground in her gymsuit outside. Fujitani-Sempai stood over her. Ishikawa-Sempai was only a second year sempai, and before Fujitani-Sempai, she was nothing.

"Sit there for the duration of practice. I

don't like to see scowling like yours as soon as I get here. So smile."

I went to the first year changing house. Everyone was undressing in silence, with laughter shaking them quietly.

"SMILE!" Fujitani-Sempai's voice rang out. Then it echoed inside the dojo, "Watanabe! Get over here!"

"Hai!" a thin voice responded.

As the practice began the sky opened and cold rain poured down; the ground beneath Ishikawa and Watanabe-Sempai turned to thick, red mud. I listened to Fujitani-Sempai, paired off with Koizumi-Sensei, screaming like someone gone mad. Had it been a real sword instead of a bamboo shinai, Koizumi-Sensei would have been dead.

When I returned finally with the bag of tangerines, I sat with Mikayo next to an electric fan looking out the window at Mrs. Yamazaki's immaculate, tiny flowergarden. A van with a loudspeaker attached crawled past outside shouting political slogans, and against the pale sky streaks of heat lightning flashed down like skeletal hands casting a spell upon the town.

Just as she reached under the cloth of my light blouse to undo the buckles of the corset, a voice called out "Gomen Kudasai!" from downstairs.

Mikayo-Sempai's eyes widened. "What is she doing?" she said aloud to herself.

The voice came again, and I recognized it as Fujitani-Sempai's voice. My heart began inexplicably to beat wildly in my chest. Although I had never been told specifically to guard the secret of my elusive friendship with Mikayo-Sempai, I somehow knew instinctively that I was expected to. We had never spoken about it, but we both knew it was not usual. If not for her accident, she would never have been so accessible to me, I knew. If not for that, my devotion would have had to remain bound up in my head. Perhaps I would have suffered the way some of my classmates did, especially the ones who loved Fujitani-Sempai. As it was I still found myself crying in my sleep when I dreamed of Mikayo's graduation. There were nights I woke saturated in perspiration from a nightmare immediately forgotten, and the word graduation hovered above, wanting me to say its name. Graduation, I would murmur, and tears would spring from my eyes.

I moved toward a cupboard with wooden-slat doors. Mikayo nodded quickly and got carefully to her feet. Inside the cupboard stuffed with folded linens I immediately began to sweat profusely. It felt as if there was no air and still wearing the tight corset, I had to crouch with my arms around my knees. The corset cut deeply into me, and I felt streaks of white pain like the heat lightning snaking through me. There was no way that I could remove it without making noise in the tiny space. I could only see strips of the room through the slats of the cupboard doors, and I heard Mikayo's startled voice say,

"Chiaki!"

Sweat streamed from my hair into my eyes which blurred and smarted as if I had come up from deep in an overly chlorinated swimming pool. In no time I was completely soaked.

"Chiaki, what have you done?" Mikayo barely whispered. I cocked my head to one side.

I could make out half of Fujitani-Sempai's face, as she sat down on the tatami, the other half obscured by Mikayo's back and her shiny hair falling over her collar. Mikayo turned her head toward the window, so that I could see her cheek, and the little curl of hair at her ear gave me such a pang that my breath caught painfully in my throat. At the moment I saw the delicate curl of Mikayo's hair, I also caught sight of the fierce, tortured eyes of Fujitani-Sempai, and the thick white bandage taped to her forehead.

Mikayo reached out to touch the bandage but Fujitani-Sempai took hold of her wrist tightly. I could see the veins standing out in her large hand.

"Do you really think I can bear this?" Fujitani-Sempai said, and I felt a broiling anxiety coursing through me.

"Do you?" Her voice was unfamiliar, adult and crushing. I was reminded of the nighttime television drama with Momoe Yamaguchi and Tomokazu Miura, where Momoe, after her accident, sat so beautifully tragic in her wheelchair wearing an expression of unspeakable sadness. I pressed a hand against my left eye in order to see better through the narrow spaces between the slats.

I could see Fujitani-Sempai's brown hands grasping Mikayo's wrists which looked very thin and white in her grip. I could make out a corner of the sky through the open window.

"How can you let her force me not to see you?" Fujitani-Sempai cried. "You almost died because of me, and now you're going to just disappear like a mist while I eat myself from the inside out?"

"Don't be so dramatic," Mikayo said. "I haven't let anyone force me to do anything. You were the one who kept saying it was wrong, not me."

I lifted myself onto my toes and saw
Fujitani-Sempai violently shake her head,
pulling at her hair.

"I was afraid! Is that so terrible? I was
afraid of what it meant!"

"I was afraid too! But not enough to let it
stop me. I even told you I loved you, the day
you took me to the subconscious museum to
see the mural of the bearded snake."

I imagined a deep cavernous place hung
with bats like jewels and melodious falling
water, where a terrible cobra with a long white
beard sat in a massive coil looking down on
them in the black gallery. I could see them in
an embrace beside a subterranean pool, the
walls of the cavern shimmering in aquatic
shadows, and Mikayo's voice from all directions at once saying I love you, I love you!

"Then why won't you let me come see you,
why? Every day I die a little more because of
this insupportable silence."

"Chiaki, you were the one who said it was
wrong! Remember how guilty you were at
Takayama? How you cried and pushed me away
and I felt so dirty, as if I had forced you! You
can't imagine how I suffered over that, while
you were ignoring me day after day at school!

And then suddenly this happened to me, and I couldn't think about you. I just couldn't."

The light darkened suddenly in the room as a cloud passed over the sun. I heard the murmur of remote thunder. My discomfort was so extreme I thought I would lose consciousness. My hopeless breaths turned to panting. I saw black flashes against the white sheet over Mikayo's futon in my blurred sight. Chiaki had pushed her back onto the bed and was hovering over her. She had her head on Mikayo's breast, and then she began to rip at her cotton t-shirt. I listened to the sound of the fabric tearing, I could see Mikayo's eyes squeezed shut, and her voice protesting. But on either side of Chiaki's head I could make out Mikayo's hands, and her hands were full of passion. I leaned gently forward to alleviate some of the burden of my own weight, sweat running like sad tears into my eyes and over my face. I couldn't break away from the cloudy vision through the slats, and in the heat I began to shake all over with chills.

I could see their faces, pressed together, and their disappeared hands reached into my imagination like windchimes. The thunder burst forth outside and the rains came crashing down. There *were* windchimes, like ice thrown over a frozen lake, like beautifully breaking windows in the strong wind. The room turned

201

suddenly white, illuminating the half naked bodies of my two upperclassmen as if in a strange dream. There were nights when I had dreamed such violent and lovely pictures. I found my hand resting against my thigh, and my mouth filled with shame and sweetness.

I remember the day she left to go to Tokyo. She had passed her exams in spite of every obstacle there was. She was going to the university. "I'm deformed now," she said. "I am a hunchback."

"You are very beautiful," I told her. We could have never been ordinary friends after everything she showed me. It won't matter if I never see you again, I will always have what you taught me, I was thinking on the day she left. Anything was possible, anything.

"Don't drink so much, Hiromi," she said to me. "I know you're doing it. I know a lot more things than you would guess."

I looked into her black eyes. They did not reflect light, and a fist closed around my heart and shook it as I held to them with my own in the tiny garden. I wish you would give me a kiss, I was thinking, just one, just one. She leaned and pressed her cheek briefly against mine, and I felt an almost imperceptible bliss descending all around me which evaporated as soon as it met my skin.

"Be a good girl, study hard and practice hard," she said, tapping my chin. She was big again.

I had rolled out of the closet when the door downstairs closed. I could hear Chiaki's footsteps on the walkway, and drops of water falling from the leaves of the little trees around the garden. The rain had stopped and I was wringing wet where I lay on the tatami breathless. I looked to Mikayo and met her eyes. She didn't look away, there was a miraculous absence of shame as we both lay exhausted, looking at each other. Then she waved me over with a limp hand. Her lips were open, as if she might say something, but she didn't. I crawled over to her and she pulled my silver buckles one by one free.

GLOSSARY OF JAPANESE WORDS

anpan	sweet bread
atari	bull's eye
biwa	a stringed instrument, like a lute
bento	a box lunch
busu	an ugly girl
enka	more traditional-style Japanese singing
furoshiki	a cloth wrapper

gaijin	foreigner, outsider
geta	wooden clogs
gomen kudasai	a greeting used when entering someone's house
hakama	long, skirt-like half of kendo-gi
happi coat	a festive jacket
hijiki	cooked seaweed
irashyai	a welcome greeting used by stores, bars etc.
janken	paper-rock-scissors game
janome	a paper umbrella
kakkoii	groovy
kampai	cheers
kendo	Japanese fencing

kendo-bu	afterschool kendo club
kendo-gi	training wear
kendo-jo	training gym
kissaten	tearoom or coffee house
kotatsu	a table warmed from beneath by coal, later by heatlamp
kukicha	tea
Mainichi Shimbun	Daily Paper
nashi	fruit like an apple and pear combined
noh	classical theatre
obi	sash of the kimono
oden	Japanese hotch-potch
ohimesama	empress
okama	fag, queen, mary

207

onibaba	demon granny
sempai	a senior, an elder
sensei	teacher, doctor
shinai	bamboo sword
shinkansen	bullet train
Takarazuka	all-female theatre, very glitzy and glam
tennisu-bu	afterschool tennis club
yaku	heroin
yakuza	gangster
yojohan	a four-and-one-half tatami size room
yukata	lightweight kimono

RADIOTEXT(E)
Neil Strauss & Dave Mandl, eds.

SEMIOTEXT(E) CANADAS
Jordan Zinovich, ed.

▲ SEMIOTEXT(E) FOREIGN AGENTS SERIES ▲
Jim Fleming & Sylvère Lotringer, Editors

POPULAR DEFENSE & ECOLOGICAL STRUGGLES
Paul Virilio

SIMULATIONS
Jean Baudrillard

GERMANIA
Heiner Müller

COMMUNISTS LIKE US
Félix Guattari & Toni Negri

ECSTASY OF COMMUNICATION
Jean Baudrillard

IN THE SHADOW OF THE SILENT MAJORITIES
Jean Baudrillard

FORGET FOUCAULT
Jean Baudrillard

REMARKS ON MARX
Michel Foucault

STILL BLACK, STILL STRONG
Dhoruba Bin Wahad, Mumia Abu-Jamal & Assata Shakur

SADNESS AT LEAVING
Erje Ayden

LOOKING BACK ON THE END OF THE WORLD
Jean Baudrillard, Paul Virilio, et al.

TAZ: The Temporary Autonomous Zone, Ontological
Anarchy, Poetic Terrorism
Hakim Bey

This Is Your Final Warning!
Thom Metzger

First and Last Emperors:
The Absolute State & the Body of the Despot
Kenneth Dean & Brian Massumi

Warcraft
Jonathan Leake

This World We Must Leave and Other Essays
Jacques Camatte

Spectacular Times
Larry Law

Future Primitive and Other Essays
John Zerzan

Wiggling Wishbone
Stories of Patasexual Speculation
Bart Plantenga

The Electronic Disturbance
Critical Art Ensemble

Invisible Governance
The Art of African Micropolitics
David Hecht & Maliqalim Simone

Cracking the Movement
Squatting Beyond the Media
Foundation for the Advancement of Illegal Knowledge

The Lizard Club
Steve Abbott

WHORE CARNIVAL
Shannon Bell, ed.

CRIMES OF CULTURE
Richard Kostelanetz

CAPITAL AND COMMUNITY
Jacques Camatte

▲ AUTONOMEDIA BOOK SERIES ▲

THE DAUGHTER
Roberta Allen

FILE UNDER POPULAR
THEORETICAL & CRITICAL WRITINGS ON MUSIC
Chris Cutler

MAGPIE REVERIES
James Koehnline

ON ANARCHY & SCHIZOANALYSIS
Rolando Perez

GOD & PLASTIC SURGERY
MARX, NIETZSCHE, FREUD & THE OBVIOUS
Jeremy Barris

MARX BEYOND MARX
LESSONS ON THE GRÜNDRISSE
Antonio Negri

RETHINKING MARXISM
Steve Resnick & Rick Wolff, eds.

THE TOUCH
Michael Brownstein

GULLIVER
Michael Ryan

MODEL CHILDREN
INSIDE THE REPUBLIC OF RED SCARVES
Paul Thorez

SCANDAL: ESSAYS IN ISLAMIC HERESY
Peter Lamborn Wilson

THE ARCANE OF REPRODUCTION
HOUSEWORK, PROSTITUTION, LABOR & CAPITAL
Leopoldina Fortunati

CLIPPED COINS, ABUSED WORDS, CIVIL GOVERNMENT
JOHN LOCKE'S PHILOSOPHY OF MONEY
Constantine George Caffentzis

TROTSKYISM AND MAOISM
THEORY & PRACTICE IN FRANCE & THE U.S.
A. Belden Fields

FILM & POLITICS IN THE THIRD WORLD
John Downing, ed.

COLUMBUS & OTHER CANNIBALS
THE WÉTIKO DISEASE & THE WHITE MAN
Jack Forbes

CASSETTE MYTHOS
THE NEW MUSIC UNDERGROUND
Robin James, ed.

ENRAGÉS & SITUATIONISTS IN
THE OCCUPATION MOVEMENT, MAY '68
René Viénet

XEROX PIRATES
"HIGH" TECH & THE NEW COLLAGE UNDERGROUND
Autonomedia Collective, eds.

POPULAR REALITY
Irreverend David Crowbar, ed.

ZEROWORK
THE ANTI-WORK ANTHOLOGY
Bob Black & Tad Kepley, eds.

THE NEW ENCLOSURES
Midnight Notes Collective

MIDNIGHT OIL
WORK, ENERGY, WAR, 1973–1992
Midnight Notes Collective

A DAY IN THE LIFE
TALES FROM THE LOWER EAST SIDE
Alan Moore & Josh Gosniak, eds.

GONE TO CROATAN
ORIGINS OF NORTH AMERICAN DROPOUT CULTURE
James Koehnline & Ron Sakolsky, eds.

ABOUT FACE
RACE IN POSTMODERN AMERICA
Timothy Maliqalim Simone

HORSEXE
ESSAY ON TRANSSEXUALITY
Catherine Millot

FORMAT AND ANXIETY
COLLECTED ESSAYS ON THE MEDIA
Paul Goodman

THE NARRATIVE BODY
Eldon Garnet

THE DAMNED UNIVERSE OF CHARLES FORT
Louis Kaplan, ed.

BY ANY MEANS NECESSARY
OUTLAW MANIFESTOS & EPHEMERA 1965–70
Peter Stansill & David Zane Mairowitz, eds.